"You're ne

"On my death
just-married b

Russell pointed a lateral finger at him as he and his bride departed for their honeymoon. "Mark my words. Some lovely damsel will bowl you over."

"Bowl me over," Drake muttered under his breath. "Only if I'm reborn a bowling pin."

He looked back at the chapel where his bowled-over buddy had just been hitched. Above the front doors were twinkling lights that outlined the words Last Stop For Love.

An appropriate name for a wedding chapel, he thought wryly. And last stop for fun, for sanity, for freedom.

Drake turned to leave when—smash!

Some thing—body—crashed into him. A shriek mingled with his grunt as he teetered for balance. White frothy material blocked his vision. He grabbed for the...bride?

"They'll be here any moment!" she exclaimed, waving her hands. "They want to kill me! Please, I need help."

The plaintive plea for his help got his attention. He couldn't turn his back on a damsel in distress any more than he could make it snow in Vegas.

"Quick." She jerked her gaze to the chapel. "We'll go in—pretend we're getting married."

Dear Reader,

We have two very different but equally enjoyable LOVE & LAUGHTER stories this month.

Bestselling Harlequin Romance author Patricia Knoll pens #53 *Delightful Jones,* a charming tale of a butler on an Arizona ranch. The last thing cowboy Tyler Morris thinks his home needs is a butler. The fact that the butler is female only makes matters worse. His ranch is for cattle and horses, not champagne and caviar. But Erin Jones is determined to do the job for which she was hired. A battle of sexes and life-styles ensues!

Then for a complete change of pace, enjoy a real screwball romance, #54 *Right Chapel, Wrong Couple* by Colleen Collins. Set in Las Vegas, it features a runaway bride, an impromptu wedding, gangsters, jewels, showgirls and just about everything else! America On Line, Romance Reader had this to say about Colleen's first book. "Some of the Love & Laughter books are destined to be classics. Colleen Collins's new book (*Right Chest, Wrong Name*) is going to be remembered for having some of the most humorous, genuinely witty lines around. Her use of dialogue, sharp and crisp, is going to be remembered, too. Frankly, I am in awe. This author is a rising star."

Have a good time and enjoy both books!

Malle Vallik

Malle Vallik
Associate Senior Editor

RIGHT CHAPEL, WRONG COUPLE
Colleen Collins

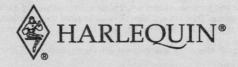

TORONTO • NEW YORK • LONDON
AMSTERDAM • PARIS • SYDNEY • HAMBURG
STOCKHOLM • ATHENS • TOKYO • MILAN • MADRID
PRAGUE • WARSAW • BUDAPEST • AUCKLAND

ISBN 0-373-44054-5

RIGHT CHAPEL, WRONG COUPLE

Printed in U.S.A.

A funny thing happened...

As a kid, I remember my dad hiding scary books from me, claiming I shouldn't read them because I had an "overactive" imagination. Of course, I'd find the books and read them anyway. And then I'd imagine stories even more elaborate and wild than what I had read! I *still* have an overactive imagination...but now I funnel my dreams and fantasies into writing my favorite type of story: romance.

For this story, because of my visits to a "gentlemen's club" (in Denver, to do research for the showgirls' dressing room, attire, etc.) I now have a VIP pass to the club!

Colleen Collins

Books by Colleen Collins

HARLEQUIN LOVE & LAUGHTER
26—RIGHT CHEST, WRONG NAME

Don't miss any of our special offers. Write to us at the following address for information on our newest releases.

Harlequin Reader Service
U.S.: 3010 Walden Ave., P.O. Box 1325, Buffalo, NY 14269
Canadian: P.O. Box 609, Fort Erie, Ont. L2A 5X3

In loving memory to my mother,
Dorothy Mary Ann Day Collins.
Thank you for everything, Mom.

1

ONLY THE DESPERATE got married in Sin City, Drake Hogan thought as he stepped from the air-conditioned Las Vegas wedding chapel into the broiling, early evening July sunshine. The heat seeped from the sidewalk through the bottoms of his wing tip shoes. He unbuttoned his rented tux jacket and offered a small prayer of thanks that he'd left the chapel as best man and not as groom.

Professional bachelor was, after all, his calling card in life.

Shrugging off his jacket, Drake watched his buddy's new bride, Liz—in a short white bridal gown and thigh-high white boots—straddle the seat of her rose-stenciled Harley. She patted the pastel leather seat behind her and winked saucily at her new husband, Russell.

"Hop on, baby," she said in a husky, come-hither voice. "It's time to start our Vegas honeymoon."

Even though most people could barely walk in this heat, Russell hopped. Drake, unbuttoning his shirt cuffs, decided marriage made one oblivious to extreme weather conditions. No one would ever make *him* hop in one-hundred-plus degree heat.

Settling onto the Harley behind his wife, Russell glanced over his shoulder. "You're next, Drake."

"On my deathbed, buddy."

Russell pointed a fateful finger at him. "Mark my words. Some lovely damsel will bowl you over."

The Harley roared to life. Russell grinned knowingly at his friend, then turned around and hugged his bride's slim hips. The Harley lurched from the curb and into traffic.

Drake loosened his tie. "Bowl me over," he muttered under his breath. "Only if I'm reborn as a bowling pin."

He looked back at the chapel where his bowled-over buddy had just been hitched. Above the front doors, which were sprayed a tacky metallic color, were twinkling lights that outlined the words *Last Stop for Love.*

An appropriate name for a wedding chapel, he thought wryly. And last stop for fun, for sanity, for freedom.

He looked back at Las Vegas Boulevard and watched the Harley weave into traffic. A flash of sunlight glinted off chrome before the bike disappeared in front of a van. Disappeared. Just like his buddy Russell had forever disappeared from single life.

I'm the last of a dying breed. The professional bachelor.

Rolling up a sleeve, Drake wondered where he could celebrate his distinguished status with a cool, soothing glass of French Chablis. Inhaling the stench of heat and asphalt, he looked above the buzzing traffic to a string of billboards that advertised everything from big-paying slot machines to half-dressed showgirls. He smiled to himself. With the former, he didn't gamble his money; with the latter, he didn't gamble his heart.

Chablis? Nah, he needed something with a kick. Like a Stinger. After all, this was Vegas. Sin City. He should order something that would slam his head and rock his gut as a tribute to his buddy's marital demise. Something like—

Smash!

Something—some*body*—crashed into him. A shriek mingled with his grunt as he teetered for balance. White frothy material blocked his vision. He flailed. His fingers caught in…hair? He smelled perfume. Roses.

The scent stayed with him as he tumbled backward onto the sidewalk.

The hard sidewalk.

The hard, hot sidewalk.

He gasped for air. Which wasn't easy considering a body was smothering him. He brushed a handful of curls from his face and met a pair of liquid brown eyes. They blinked at him in surprise.

"I'm—" she panted "—sorry." An amber curl tumbled over her brow. She winced. "My knee hurts."

He started to say, "My entire body hurts," but she shifted, causing her elbow to wedge into his solar plexus. He gasped instead, then he felt the heat of the sidewalk like a hot iron permanently melding his shirt to his back.

She squirmed off him and jumped to her feet, then seemed to be running without getting anywhere. At first Drake thought the concrete was too hot, until he realized she was unsure where to go.

Raising himself onto one elbow, he groped for his jacket and watched the blur of her dancing form. Obviously her knee was better.

Struggling for breath, he stared at her active feet, the sight of which stunned him almost more than the recent body collision had. At first he thought her feet had been dipped in fairy dust, but then realized her sneakers were covered with rhinestones. Topping her glittering shoes were socks that resembled antique hankies.

His gaze traveled up a pair of the longest legs he'd ever seen. Slim and tanned. Legs that continued to dance frantically. And he thought Russell had been crazy to hop in this heat. This woman made hopping look like a stroll.

"They'll be here any moment!" she exclaimed, waving her hands.

Staggering to his feet, he eyed her dress—layers of lacy material with pieces of knickknacks sewn in. It definitely matched her shoe style.

Breathing in a stream of molten air, his first full breath, Drake managed to sputter, "Who's—they?"

"Quick!" Her hands were waving so fast he thought for sure she'd take off in flight. "We have to do something!" She jerked her gaze to the chapel. "A chapel! Ugh, not again. No, perfect!" She stopped dancing and bestowed a look of approval on Drake. "We'll go in—pretend we're getting married."

Pretend?

He was already in a tux; she was in some Star Trek bridal ensemble. The delicate rose scent now smelled suspiciously like eau de wedding. As in "setup." Like the time a former girlfriend had surprised her entire family—and him—by introducing him as her fiancé at Thanksgiving dinner. After his adamant denial, the family had treated him like a bigger turkey than the main course.

Holding up his hands in a truce, Drake began backing down the sidewalk. Safety was a mere dash down the alley to his trusty '58 'Vette, the only object of his affection.

"Nice, uh, running into you, but I have to walk my dog." A getaway line he'd used a hundred times. He attempted a half smile. *Don't make any sudden movements. She's a bride-to-be on the edge.* Turning slowly, he started to walk away.

"They're…going to kill me."

He stopped.

"Please," she said softly. "I need help."

The plaintive plea for his help got his attention. He couldn't turn his back on a damsel in distress any more than he could make it snow in Vegas. He turned around.

Ms. Rhinestone Shoes, for a change, stood still, her big brown eyes filling with tears.

"Kill?" he repeated.

"They'll kill me." She looked around. "I'm stuck at the end of the Strip. My only chance is if that gas station bathroom is unlocked—" she gestured across Las Vegas Boulevard to a lone filling station with a green dinosaur logo "—I transform myself into a cactus or we go into this chapel.…"

Those beseeching, big brown eyes finished her sentence. She still wanted him to "pretend" to marry her.

He should leave this bizarre scene. But her vulnerability—her neediness—tugged at his gut. He felt responsible to help her just as he had every time one of his four younger sisters had needed their big brother's help.…

But she's not my sister.

She's a strange woman who wants to drag me into a wedding chapel.

"I'm not getting hitched—"

"And I'm not *proposing*." Her eyes flashed. "What do you think? That every woman's dream is to have a ring on her finger? Men," she muttered. Pivoting, she loped up the steps and into Last Stop for Love, her rhinestone shoes sparkling all the way.

Drake swiped at his brow. He could still sprint for the Corvette. Leave behind this wacky damsel in distress. But just as he heard the chapel doors shut crisply behind her, he spied two guys walking purposefully down the sidewalk toward him. He might have ignored them, thinking they were tourists, except both were dressed in dark suits—hardly what anyone in his right mind wore in near-hell heat. That both also wore dark shades gave them a mutant Blues Brothers look.

The only difference in their attire was the gaudy Hawaiian shirt the short one wore under his suit jacket. The tall one stuck with button-down white.

Drake would have split, except he didn't like how they were glancing from left to right, obviously searching for something.

Ms. Rhinestone Shoes?

Despite the heat, his insides chilled. Maybe she'd told the truth. Maybe she was in danger.

His big-brother instincts kicked in. He couldn't leave her alone to face these gangster types.

Trying to look nonchalant, he slung the jacket over his shoulder and ambled up the steps, humming to himself. Using his peripheral vision, he decided the thugs were a good fifty feet away. They'd probably think he was a groom-to-be, heading toward his wedding day. Drake tried to look happy.

He slipped inside the chapel doors, grateful for the rush of air-conditioning. The interior was just as it had been when he'd first stepped in here for Russell's wedding a mere hour ago. In the alcove were several overstuffed white couches, a register, a drinking fountain. And the most hideous carpet he'd ever seen. He'd already decided it had once been gold, but the tread of hundreds of lovesick feet had dimmed its luster.

Not unlike what happens to marriages.

Standing in line behind two closed doors—upon which

hung a sign saying Please Wait, the Minister Will Be with You—were several soon-to-be-married couples. Well, several couples and one forlorn-looking woman dressed in a godawful wedding dress.

Sidling up next to her, Drake slipped his jacket onto her shoulders. "Better cover up. Two mafioso types are cruising the street. Know them?"

She stiffened. "Did one have big cheeks?"

He frowned, trying to remember. "The short one had a roundish face and a hideous Hawaiian shirt. His buddy was tall."

"That's them," she said, her voice rising to a squeak. "I'm dead. I should have just let them take me to another chapel, but no, I had to jump out of the car and run away—" she looked around, tears welling in her eyes "—to Last Stop for Love. Or Last Stop for Life, if these guys get their way."

"Another chapel?"

Fancy Shoes blinked back the tears. "I was supposed to get married, but I escaped." Her voice dropped to a shaky whisper. "I wouldn't put it past Grave's thugs to kill me now."

Escaping matrimony was something to be celebrated, Drake thought, not something to kill over. This Grave fellow needed to get out more or stop taking rejection personally. Trying to think of something comforting to say, Drake patted her hand. It was ice-cold. She needed more than soothing words to dispel her terror.

"Let me check outside," he said. "Maybe they're gone."

He crossed to the window and stared through the filmy, gold-threaded curtains at the stretch of gray sidewalk just as the thugsters strode past. She was right. The short one looked like a chipmunk that had stored too many nuts in his cheeks. The tall one had a blank look that matched his nondescript white shirt.

Drake crossed back to her. In a reassuring voice, he said, "They're walking down the street. Maybe they'll keep going."

"Hardly. They know I have to be in that gas station across the street or in this chapel." Her small chin quivered as her brown eyes met his. "I should have had the operation to begin with, but no-o-o, I refused. Then Grave got it into his head that if he was my husband, he could force the operation. The thugs were taking me to some chapel to meet him, but at a red light, I escaped."

"Operation?"

"Grave had until noon tomorrow to connect with some muck-a-muck out of state who wanted the, uh..." She shot a suspicious look at Drake. "But thanks to my jumping ship, that deal's probably off. Although if Grave finds me and drags me into a marriage, I suppose the deal's on again. But on *or* off, I still have the debt to settle."

"Debt?"

In a zombielike monotone, she finished, "Now I'll never be a reflexologist."

Reflexologist? Debt? Operation? Drake had opened his mouth to ask any one of the hundred questions that crowded his mind when the couple in front of them started arguing, their words thick with booze.

"Can't shee." The woman pulled off her veil, taking her hairpiece with it. "What'sh thish cat doing on my veil?" she asked, staring bleary-eyed at the hairpiece.

A woman who looked as though she'd stepped out of the painting *American Gothic* approached the drunken couple. Drake remembered her from Russell's wedding. She was the manager of the Last Stop for Love, her job to ensure that couples moved in and out promptly. She was foreman of this wedding assembly line.

After a dignified sniff, she said to the drunken couple, "You two must leave. We don't perform weddings for intoxicated people."

The man held up a piece of paper. "We have a lishensh."

American Gothic arched one penciled-in eyebrow. "To-morrow we'd love to see you. But not today."

The man sputtered something, took his lady friend by the elbow and steered her toward the front doors. As they passed, the woman tossed her veil, hair and all, at the two couples in line.

Ms. Rhinestone Shoes caught it.

The drunken woman laughed and told her groom-to-be, "She caught the cat."

They staggered out the door, holding on to each other.

Drake spied something on the floor. He picked it up. "Their license," he said, straightening. "I'll return it—"

"No." Rhinestone Shoes turned those liquid brown eyes on him with full-force intensity. From the veil she was holding, she tugged the hairpiece and tossed it into a corner trash can. Adjusting the veil on her head, she added, "We might need it."

"But it—"

"Looks legit. Keep holding it." She pulled the gauzy material around her face. "How do I look?"

"Like a rent-a-bride."

"Close enough. Hold my hand."

He hesitated.

"It's a rent-a-hand, not the real thing." She grasped his fingers. "If those guys show up, we'll look like two everyday people, madly in love, ready to get married."

Madly in love? He'd never experienced that. But if the gist of her story was real—that her life was in danger—he could fake it.

She looked around the room, peering intently through the gauzy veil. "There's got to be another way out."

"There is. Behind the pulpit in the chapel."

She flashed him a questioning look.

"I was just in there a few minutes ago, watching my best buddy get married." Drake gestured to his clothes. "Trust me. I only rent tuxes under duress—this isn't my idea of leisure wear."

She looked him up and down. "You don't need to tell me that's rented."

He was momentarily speechless. Ms. Rhinestone Shoes, wearing something that looked as though it were leased for Halloween, dared to say he looked *rented?*

"Only the best dressers can pull that off," she added. "You know, wearing something rented."

As he debated whether his ego felt deflated or inflated, American Gothic ushered the couple in front of them into the chapel. While taped organ music swelled, Drake checked out his companion with the knack for backhanded compliments.

Through the veil, he searched her big brown eyes. She had a way of widening them as though a thought had just surprised her. Framing her face was a mass of brown curls that looked as though they needed taming.

Like her, no doubt.

He didn't know how long he'd been staring at her when she suddenly put her head on his shoulder and wrapped an arm around his waist. The netting rustled as she whispered, "I heard the doors open. Are they here?"

He shifted his gaze past her veil-topped curls. Sure enough, the two thugs were closing the door behind them as they scanned the alcove.

Drake averted his eyes and pretended to stare lovingly at a sequin on the net.

"Next?" said a familiar scratchy voice.

American Gothic looked at him primly. Behind her, a couple flushed from reciting their vows almost skipped from the chapel to the front doors.

American Gothic's eyebrow arched a notch as she recognized him. "You were just in here."

One of the thugs was walking their way, Drake saw from the corner of his eye. He had to save the girl.

"Always the best man, never the groom," he quipped. "Until now."

He turned to his bride-to-be. "Darling," he said in his best I-love-you voice—a voice he normally reserved for let's-go-to-the-bedroom, not let's-go-into-the-chapel. "We're next." He put his arm around her, his hand blocking her profile as best he could.

Darting a glance behind him, Drake saw the chipmunk-cheeked thug eyeing them. His buddy was admiring an Elvis painting on black velvet that hung on the back wall.

American Gothic turned, indicating with a flourish of her bony hand that Drake and Rhinestones Shoes were to follow.

With a jerky motion, she opened two doors—painted the same tacky metallic hue as the outside doors—and, with an authoritative dip of her head, motioned them forward.

Once inside the chapel, she closed the doors behind them and clasped her hands. "Do you want the 'Wedding March' or 'I'll Be Loving You'?"

"'Wedding March,'" Drake answered. *Which we'll do right past the minister and out that back door.*

She turned and shoved a cassette into a tape player. Taking advantage of the manager's diverted attention, Drake grabbed his bride-to-be and pulled her along the dirty gold carpet. The minister, looking as dour as before, stood on a raised platform at the back of the church and squirted breath freshener into his mouth.

Drake and his almost-bride approached the pulpit at breakneck speed. The minister, dressed in a gray suit that matched his ring of frizzy gray hair, froze in mid-freshener-squirt and blinked.

"Whoa, there." He made a halting motion, like a traffic cop. "This is a wedding, children, not a fire."

"It is for us," Ms. Rhinestones Shoes said.

As Drake skidded to a stop, nearly tripping his almost-bride, the chapel doors creaked open. He glanced over his shoulder. Chipmunk Cheeks stood in the back. His small eyes compressed into glittering slits as he seemed to recognize the girl.

Drake tightened his grip on her elbow. Better to play this one out and hope for the best. He checked out the area behind the pulpit. Ten feet away was the door he remembered. He glanced down. A thin line of sunlight illuminated the floor; the door led outside. Good. Drake eased out a pent-up breath as he returned his gaze to the minister, who cleared his throat.

"The journey of your life together begins with this first step," he began in a serious monotone.

Drake slid another glance over his shoulder. The short thug, catching his eye, pulled back his jacket to reveal a holster and a gun.

"Your witnesses may come forward," the minister said.

Drake jerked his gaze back to the minister. "Witnesses?" he hissed.

"Witnesses?" repeated Ms. Rhinestone Shoes, wide-eyed.

"They're not our witnesses," said Drake quickly, putting a protective arm around her. Against the length of his body, he could feel her shaking. She'd been right. He had to get them out of here before the wedding march became the death march.

"In fact," he continued in his best buddy-to-buddy voice, "my fiancée and I never met them before today. They're—they're a...gay couple who followed us inside. Said they were...chapel shopping for their upcoming wedding. Bugged us for a lot of wedding tips—you know, where to register, where to honeymoon."

He was so deep into lies, he might as well go for broke. Nuzzling his almost-bride, he said solemnly, "She's pregnant and not feeling well. Can we speed this up?"

"Preg—?" Ms. American Gothic seemed unable to finish the *P* word. "I'll be your witness," she added matter-of-factly. "Besides, we don't do mixed marriages." She glanced at the tent dress. "A woman with child, yes." She looked knowingly back into Drake's eyes. "But *mixed*, no."

Mixed? She made the Blues Brothers sound like a cocktail. Drake had a momentary urge to explain the difference between mixed and same-sex couples to her, but she was already taking matters in hand.

Holding up one stiff palm to the thugs, she said loudly, "You two...fellows...must wait outside. You can talk to the couple *after* they're married."

After some muttering and scuffling of feet, Drake heard the chapel doors open and close. The minister, now looking more surprised than dour, was staring at the bride-to-be's stomach. Drake followed his line of vision. Her lacy, layered dress was shapeless—she could be anything in that getup. Pregnant. A basketball smuggler. And nobody would be the wiser.

"The license?" asked the minister, extending his hand.

Drake handed over the license with the two strangers' names. The lies about the thugs were bad enough. But lying about his identity—to a man of the cloth—made him feel guiltier than the time Father O'Brien had caught Drake-the-Altar-Boy imbibing communion wine.

Reading the license, the minister said, "Harriet and Rudolpho, welcome to Last Stop for Love—"

Harriet and Rudolpho? Drake pictured the drunken couple. They sounded like a doughnut-maker and a flamenco dancer.

"I think I feel contractions," interrupted Harriet. Underneath the veil, she winked at Drake.

"Yes," Drake concurred, looking back at the minister. "We don't want the baby born *here*—"

"We'd have to name it Last Stop," finished Harriet. "People will think she was born in a train station." She groaned again, obviously for good measure.

She? That was a little presumptuous. But despite the circumstances, Drake had to stop himself from grinning. *Last Stop.* Harriet's sense of humor didn't fail her, even in a crisis.

"Good heavens." The minister fumbled with the Bible and began rapidly reciting the wedding vows. When there was a pause, Drake took his cue.

"I do," he said.

"I was speaking to Harriet."

"I do," she answered, wincing slightly.

Drake frowned at her. She was *wincing?* Had to be acting out more contractions. No woman, after all, had ever experienced *pain* at the notion of marrying *him.*

"Rudolpho?" the minister queried.

Drake turned away from his bride's scrunched face. "I do?"

"You may now kiss the bride."

He was accustomed to kisses at a lady's door, kisses on her couch, kisses on the way to her bedroom, but never in his wildest dreams had he imagined he'd be kissing anyone in front of a minister after being pronounced man and wife.

What had he done?

His thought was cut short by the hesitant touch of soft lips against his cheek.

He turned slightly and met those lips. Warm. Sweet. The kiss took him by surprise with its simple intensity. He looked into sable eyes. A scent of roses teased his senses. She had pulled back the veil and, for the first time today, he had a long moment to look at her.

She appeared to be in her early thirties, although a naiveté in her gaze made her seem younger. Her face was heart shaped, her skin lightly tanned. And those eyes... They were so big he swore he could read her soul within them. She smiled—an infectious grin that could soften the hardest heart.

The minister cleared his throat.

Her lips parted.

So did Drake's.

"Tip the man," she whispered.

"Tip," he repeated, too dazed to comprehend the meaning of the word.

"Tip. As in money." She grinned again.

"Tip. Yes." Without breaking their gaze, Drake fished in his pants pocket and extracted a bill. He shoved it into the minister's outstretched hand.

Something thumped against the closed chapel doors in the back—followed by a cold thump of reality in Drake's chest. *The thugs.* He had to get Harriet out of here. *Now.*

Drake shoved another bill into the minister's palm. "Stop that gay couple from following us."

The minister, pocketing the money, nodded to Drake before heading up the aisle toward the chapel doors.

Squeezing his bride's hand, Drake leaped toward the pulpit.

"Where are you going?" Ms. American Gothic asked, her voice rising an octave. "The doors are the other way—"

He yanked on Harriet. With a squeal, she stumbled after him.

"Good heavens, be careful with the mother-to-be," cried Ms. American Gothic.

"She's a broodmare—grew up on a farm," Drake called over his shoulder. Dragging his bride behind him, he ran around the pulpit and shoved open the door. A blast of fiery air greeted them. He swung Harriet in front of him and gave her a hearty push outside. "Let's get the hell out of here!" he yelled as he slammed the door.

They were in an alley. The July heat felt like a sauna after the cool temperature of the chapel. On the far side of the alley, a wino leaned against a dented green dumpster. He saluted them with his bottle. "Besh wishes!" He took a slug.

Harriet turned to Drake, handing him his jacket. A slight breeze lifted her veil. "I can get home from here. Thanks for...marrying me."

To his surprise, she started jogging away. He ran behind her and caught her arm.

"You marry me, then leave me?" he asked, halting her progress.

"I'm not *using* you." She flashed him an exasperated look. "Men! Such fragile egos!"

He ignored her. "I'll drive you to your car."

"No car."

"I'll drive you home, then." He slipped on the jacket he was holding and gently pulled her toward the chapel parking lot.

She resisted. "I don't want to get into some strange car. I don't know you!"

"You don't know me, but you married me." Pulling her along, Drake gave his head a shake.

"With that bogus license, we're not *legally* married, you know."

"You wish."

"I wish *what?*" When he didn't answered, she sputtered, "What an ego!"

"It's fragile, remember?"

She squirmed against his hold. "I'll—I'll take a bus."

"Dressed like that?" He gave a yank. She half stumbled behind him. "People will think you're an escapee from Disneyland."

"Disneyland—?" She snorted. "I *made* this dress, I'll have you know!"

"You made a wedding dress for a marriage you didn't want?"

"Of course not. It's not a wedding dress. It just happens to be white," she replied indignantly.

"How foolish of me," Drake mumbled sarcastically.

"And I resent that farm remark," she added. "Broad mare—"

"*Brood* mare. I was winging it—"

"I've lived—in Vegas—all my life," she said between pants. "Hardly the place to learn about—moody horses."

He flashed her an exasperated look. "Hustle it up," he said. "Women," he added under his breath.

"Women," echoed the wino as they passed. "Can't live wish 'em, can't kill 'em."

Kill.

She had been afraid they'd kill her.

Drake broke into a jog, forcing his bride to do the same. "Up here," he yelled over his shoulder, indicating the parking lot with a jerk of his head. Rounding the corner, he dragged her behind him and all but pushed her toward his convertible, a cherry red, classic Corvette. With a yell—"Jump!"—he half tossed her over the door and into the passenger seat before bounding to the driver's side. Opening the door, he hopped in and slammed it shut.

Swiping at the sweat on her forehead, she glared at him. "You throw me in, but open the door for yourself?"

He barely glanced in her direction while twisting the ignition key. "What do you think this is—a date?"

She blew out a gust of air. "You wish. What time is it?"

He sent her a disbelieving look before he flicked his wrist. "Almost eight." He glanced back up. "Where to?"

Before she could answer, a throaty male voice barked, "There she is!"

Simultaneously, they turned around. Running from the alley into the parking lot, the chipmunk-cheeked thug pointed at her as his taller cohort stumbled alongside.

"Floor it!" she screamed.

2

THE GUY SHE KNEW as Rudolpho stomped on the gas. The wheels peeled rubber as the car shot forward, barely missed a green Toyota and careened toward the street. Bumping over the curb, they swerved into traffic, Rudolpho driving as though he were entering the Indy 500 instead of Las Vegas Boulevard.

Gripping the grab bar, LuLu Lewis wished fervently that she was on her trusty bike. Pedaling down a street accompanied by chirping birds was far preferable to flooring it down a street accompanied by blasting horns.

She peeked back at the parking lot. The short thug was gesturing wildly at the escaping Corvette. The tall thug was looking skyward, scratching his head. A blue-and-silver, double-decker tour bus cut off her view.

She leaned her head back and gulped a mouthful of warm air. Despite the withering heat, she felt reenergized as the Corvette put more distance between her and Grave's thugs. Plus they were heading away from the Strip. Although Rudolpho didn't know, it was a good move. Not only was traffic lighter, but her house was in this direction.

The house she'd lived in all her life.

The house that Gramps and Grandma Suzie had moved into after her parents' death almost thirty years ago. And because it was probably the next place Grave and his thugs would look, LuLu would have to leave it. An ache coursed through her at the thought of abandoning her home, her haven.

Moments later, the Corvette lurched to a stop at a red light. Rudolpho glared at her. "What the hell am I doing speeding through Las Vegas with a woman I just married whose name I don't even know?" He muttered something unintelligible before adding, "I never take Sylvia over sixty-five. Even on the highway."

His angry tone diverted her thoughts from home. "Sylvia?"

"My 'Vette."

It took her a moment to realize he didn't mean a veterinarian. "You named your car *Sylvia?*"

"Old girlfriend. Long story."

She looked at the spotless leather upholstery and the shiny dash panel. "She must have had a great interior."

"Exterior, actually."

LuLu didn't know what was worse—the heat, the near escape or the macho conversation.

"I'm in a bad dream, right?" she said, tapping her fingers on Sylvia's leather seat. "One where I'm being chased by thugs after marrying a stereotypical male who's more interested in a woman's outside than her insides." She sighed deeply. "The only thing to make this nightmare perfect is to discover I'm also naked."

He opened his mouth to say something, but the light changed. She was grateful for the roar of the motor—it prevented further conversation about Sylvia's exterior.

LuLu folded her arms tightly under her chest. Just her luck to be saved by a knight in shining armor with a pickup-bar mentality. Although she loved Vegas, loved the desert, she hated the caliber of men this town attracted. It was a Mecca for Neanderthal "me-man, you-chick" attitudes.

At the next red light, while shifting gears, he asked, "What's your name?"

She fought the urge to answer "Sylvia." "Louise Lewis. But people call me LuLu." She dragged her hand through her windblown curls. She probably looked like Orphan Annie on crack. "You?"

"Drake Hogan. People call me Drake." He slid her a glance. "I caught a few key words before, but I still don't get why these guys want to kill you."

"Because I didn't marry their boss."

"You got cold feet?"

"In this weather?" She sighed heavily. "Let's just say that

I wouldn't agree to an operation. Those thugs would just as soon shoot me and cart me back to Grave's doctor to get the—the... To sum it up, I have something Grave wants.'' She didn't know this guy sitting next to her. It'd be stupid to spill any info about the diamond—what if he, too, decided to kill her? As insane as the thought was, her better instincts told her that a little explanation was better than too much. She'd long ago learned to watch out for Number One.

"So you wouldn't have the operation, you wouldn't marry him and he's decided to kill you. He wants it that bad?''

The tenderness in Drake's voice momentarily unnerved her. "Yep,'' she answered, trying to sound tougher than she felt. "Nothing like being wanted.'' Ignoring his perplexed look, she dipped her head toward the light. "It's green.''

They sped off. She wanted to yell directions to her house, but knew her words would be eaten by blasts of scorching air. Instead, she hunkered down and debated her current situation. *Maybe I should have married Grave.* She looked out at the passing cars, heat baked on the outside, coolly air-conditioned on the inside. Similar to how she felt right now—uncomfortably hot yet chilled with fear. *But now Grave thinks I'm married to somebody else and he has no legal means to force the operation. He'll kill me for sure. Why didn't I just go with the program?*

She peeked over the seat at the traffic behind them.

No sign of Grave's thugs.

Yet, anyway.

The Corvette pulled to another stop. In the distance a smattering of twinkling lights dotted the desert terrain. Not too many people knew that beyond the bright lights of Sin City lay the hazy glow of a sprawling suburbia. She remembered the tourist who was agog that LuLu had grown up watching TV and riding a tricycle. He'd thought Las Vegas kids grew up watching lounge acts and hailing cabs.

Drake's voice interrupted her thoughts. "What kind of car do the Blues Brothers drive?'' He peered into his rearview mirror.

"Blues Brothers?''

"The goons."

She pulled a curl out of her face before answering. "Gold Chevy with big chrome headlights. Named Madonna."

"They named their car Madonna?" he asked, surprised.

"Nope. I did. Figured it was a good exterior nickname."

"Madonna," he murmured, pulling a toothpick from his shirt pocket. "Touché." He popped the toothpick into his mouth.

Gesturing at the street ahead, she said, "Turn left at the next light. My house is about five miles from here."

"Do these guys know where you live?"

"Yes."

"Then why—?"

"Because I have to pick up Gramps."

She swallowed back a lump in her throat. A lot was at stake. Her life. Maybe Gramps's. Her home. If Grave caught up with her, he'd demand, among other things, for her to repay the debt. If he didn't accept a payment plan, she'd have no choice but to sign over her house. Which meant signing over a life-time of memories. Gramps parading around the kitchen in an apron, concocting some new chocolate-drizzled recipe; Suzie decorating the Christmas tree with her crocheted snowflakes....

Of course, when Suzie got sick, she hadn't been able to do much needlework. LuLu and Gramps had made her sewing room into a makeshift hospital room. Most of the caretaking had fallen on LuLu, but it was a labor of love. Her grand-mother's last days were spent surrounded by family and warmth, not by strangers in a cold hospital. Afterward, LuLu and Gramps had turned the room into a nursery, filled with all the plants Suzie had loved.

LuLu ached at the thought of never walking through that room again, smelling the fresh scent of flowers. Or never again sitting with Gramps in the backyard, chatting about their day, their conversation punctuated by the occasional hoot of an owl.

These memories of home were the best in her life. The pain of loss rocked through her. *I can't bear it.*

She shook her head, chiding herself. Of course she could

bear it. Didn't matter if she lost everything, as long as she didn't lose Gramps. Ever since Suzie died, he was her only family, her best friend, her everything.

"I said, is that your grandfather?"

She'd been so consumed with her memories, she'd missed Drake's question. "Yes, my grandfather," she confirmed softly. "After we pick him up, if you could give us a lift, I'd appreciate it." She hated asking for favors. Usually she took care of everything herself. But that wouldn't work in this situation. Like it or not, she needed Drake's help.

He stared up at the encroaching twilight and rolled the toothpick between his lips. "Where do I take you two?"

Good question. She fingered a fringe of lace on her dress. Couldn't go to Capri, the casino where she worked, because that's where Grave was. Her best pal, Belle, lived in a studio apartment with three cats and a paranoid parakeet—there was hardly room for two more guests on the lam. Besides, LuLu didn't want to endanger another life.

She attempted a smile. "Your place?"

"My place is three hundred miles away."

"Wonderful." Her stomach plummeted. "I'm saved by a man who lives on another planet."

The light flashed green. Drake shifted into first, but didn't take off. "I live in L.A., not on Mars," he said tersely, the toothpick jutting out one side of his mouth.

"Saving my life doesn't give you the right to get huffy."

Drake bit down on the toothpick as he stepped on the gas. The tires squealed. The scent of burning rubber trailed them.

She glanced over at him. It was obvious Drake Hogan was no Mario Andretti. *Keep this up and poor Sylvia will start to show her age.* Snuggling down in her seat, LuLu cast him an appraising look.

The wind blew back his dark hair, exposing a high forehead. With the last traces of sunlight, she could see that his face was tanned, rugged. He must be the kind of guy who was outside a lot. Probably from cruising in Sylvia.

Her gaze traveled down his body. Through his fitted shirt, she deciphered a nicely molded torso. A small thrill of heat that had nothing to do with the weather curled through her. She quickly looked back to his face.

And that toothpick. Had he recently quit smoking?

Her inventory was cut short as he said curtly, "You'd be huffy too if you drove six hours to Vegas—in the middle of summer with no air-conditioning—to be best man at your buddy's wedding, and ended up carpooling with two people trying to dodge Vegas mafiosi. Now, where do you live?"

Not too many men succumbed to minor emotional outbursts. Maybe, LuLu decided, Drake Hogan wasn't such a stoic Neanderthal, after all.

Through gestures and pointing, she guided him down several streets to her house, which was nestled in a suburban tract outside Vegas proper. After they pulled up in front of her ranch-style home, she jumped out of the car.

Drake was right behind her, minus the toothpick, when she reached the front door. "I've never seen a purple door before," he said.

He sounded as though he wanted to make amends. It reminded her of how her sourpuss grandfather could turn sweet when he wanted to make up with Suzie.

"Eggplant purple," LuLu explained in an equally conciliatory tone. "Or so Gramps calls it. He's the cook of the family, so I guess he sees the world through food-colored glasses." Opening the door, she stepped inside. "Babaloo! We've got to split!"

Drake followed her. "Babaloo?"

"His nickname."

The familiar rattle of the air conditioner comforted her, the cool air soothed her. She tried not to think that this might be the last time she stood in her living room. She had to think survival.

Money.

She and Gramps needed cash. She headed for the plaid couch, yanked up one of the lumpy cushions and retrieved a plastic bag filled with bills. Her secret stash had always been an antidote to Gramps's money-foolish ways.

That is, until recently. Overshooting the food budget was

peanuts compared to his surprise gambling debt at Capri. Gramps, in his single-minded pursuit, had unwittingly turned their lives upside down. Lives they might lose. Fighting a shudder, she called out again, "Babaloo!"

Drake gave his head a shake. "LuLu. Babaloo. Does anybody in Vegas have a real name?"

"Billy," answered a craggy voice.

LuLu glanced up as Gramps lumbered into the living room.

From the look on Drake's face, she knew how he was reacting to her grandfather. She'd seen it before. Gramps might be in his late seventies, but he had an imposing presence. Six-four with a face that could double for a road map, he scared little kids just by looking at them. And despite numerous discussions on haircuts, his mass of white hair always looked as though the man had been zapped with electricity. For a while he had wrestled with spray gels and hair-dryers, but eventually Gramps had given up and let his hair have its way.

His saving grace was that underneath his Frankenstein exterior, he was Betty Crocker incarnate. Today he wore a lacy white apron over his blue polyester leisure suit.

He strode forward a few steps and scrutinized Drake. "Why we got to split? Is this man from the IRS?"

"L.A.," answered Drake.

Gramps harrumphed. "That's what's wrong with the world today. IRS. L.A. Everything's abbreviated. And now we got to split ASAP."

"Babaloo," LuLu said, keeping her voice even. "Thanks to your gambling debt, we have to leave."

"Leave? I'm in the middle of hamburger surprise—"

"*Now.* Or we'll have another surprise from Grave's thugs." She knew Gramps knew exactly what she was talking about. Messing with Grave was like teasing a viper. "Drake will help you pack a few things." Motioning to Drake, she mouthed, "Help him."

Drake mouthed back, "Yeah, right," but stopped when he caught her determined look.

Gramps puffed out his cheeks, nodded briskly and turned on his heel. LuLu had seen this action a thousand times—she always figured it was a habit from his marine days. Drake, after one last thanks-a-lot look at LuLu, dutifully followed him down the hall.

A few minutes later, LuLu reentered the living room carrying her workout bag, into which she'd thrown a few clothes and miscellaneous items. There stood Gramps, looking grumpy, and Drake, looking miffed, with a faded Marine Corps duffel bag on the floor between them. Gramps had undoubtedly put Drake through a few stressful moments since the three of them had last convened.

"Let's go," said LuLu matter-of-factly, heading toward the front door.

Gramps blinked at her in surprise. "Aren't you taking Mayberry?"

LuLu stopped. "Mayberry!" She swiveled and made a bee-line toward the mantel over the mock fireplace. She scooped up an assortment of small wooden objects and dropped them into a pocket in her dress. "Okay," she said triumphantly, turning. "We can go now."

"I can't…" Gramps shook his head sadly. "I can't leave Suzie." He planted one massive hand over his heart.

"Babaloo," LuLu said softly, "we have to leave her here."

"You're taking Mayberry."

"Mayberry is small compared to Suzie."

The following moment of silence was broken only by the rattling of the air conditioner. "Who's Suzie?" Drake finally asked.

LuLu and her grandfather ignored the question. "Babaloo," she continued, "we don't have time to discuss this."

He puffed out his cheeks. "No Suzie, no Babaloo."

"No Suzie," LuLu said tightly, wishing he didn't get to her. No two-year-old could compete with her grandfather's bullheadedness.

"Then no Babaloo." Gramps crossed his arms, obviously ready to entrench in this battle of wills.

"That's it," interjected Drake, stepping between them. "Yes to Suzie. Yes yes yes. I don't care if she's a three-hundred-pound canary, we're taking her, because I don't want

the three of us standing here when the Blues Brothers decide
to pay a house call.''

LuLu sighed in resignation. ''Okay!'' She stomped back
through the living room toward the kitchen. ''Let's go get
Suzie.''

She led the way through the kitchen and out the back screen
door. The three of them stood in the backyard on a circle of
concrete bordered with an assortment of cacti. From somewhere in the encroaching darkness, an owl hooted. Lights from
the kitchen window cut a yellow rectangle across the small
yard, clearly illuminating what sat in the center of the concrete.

Drake blinked. ''*This* is Suzie?''

''Yes, this is Suzie,'' Gramps answered solemnly, his voice
cracking on the name. He sighed heavily. ''Pink was her favorite color.''

In the spill of light from the kitchen window, Drake read
the chiseled letters *S-u-z-i-e*, which were etched in a lopsided
diagonal across a pink marble headstone.

I'm in a stranger's backyard, paying homage to a rosy slab.
His heart lurched.

Slab.

''You buried her in your backyard?'' Drake rasped as he
glanced around, relieved that only cacti, and no other headstones, dotted the sparse yard. Which was in his favor. Maybe
they only buried their dearly beloveds, and not innocent
strangers who accidentally stumbled into their lives.

''It's just the headstone,'' LuLu explained in an annoyed
undertone. ''No body.''

Drake responded with a snort of disbelief. ''No body?
Where is she?''

''Whispering Meadows Cemetery,'' answered LuLu.

Whispering Meadows? He looked around. *Is that what they
call this cacti-strewn, concrete-covered backyard?*

She planted one fist on her hip. ''What do you think we
are?'' she asked, as though reading his thoughts. ''Body
snatchers?''

Yes. He was surprised the headstone was pink and not eggplant purple.

But rather than say what he was thinking, he coughed and pretended to study the star-clustered sky. In the last few hours, he'd married a stranger, escaped two members of the Vegas Godfather Club and now hung out with "Babaloo" and LuLu, fledgling morticians.

This was starting to feel like a bad *Addams Family* remake.

He looked back down, focusing on a nick at the corner of Suzie-the-Headstone. "I have to go," he said. Or meant to say. His constricted air passage warped his words into unrecognizable sounds.

LuLu dipped her head closer, the kitchen light accenting traces of gold in her hair. "You have to flow?"

"Flow, shmo," interrupted Gramps as he leaned over and laid his hands on the sides of the headstone. "Too much New Age talk these days. No marine worth his spit ever said *flow*. Piss, yes. Flow, no." He nodded authoritatively toward Drake. "Grab the other side, son, and just say it like it is."

Like it is, Drake wanted to say, *is that I want to go home. Now.*

Because if he stayed, his name would end up in some cheesy magazine story about a deranged Vegas family and their backyard headstone collection. In the story's itemization of victims, Drake Hogan would be listed as Headstone Number Five.

He looked around. Okay, Number Two.

As his gaze skimmed over the prickly silhouette of a cactus, he imagined the rest of the story. Didn't they always say something complimentary about the deceased? If so, there'd be mention that he had taught theater arts at Santa Monica Junior College. That he liked kids, young and old. That he was survived by four sisters—although the article would fail to mention the pranks and problems from which he had repeatedly rescued them. That he was survived by a best friend named Russell Harrington. Who, out of loyalty to his best bud, Drake, would insist they add that Headstone Number Two loved jazz, tennis and fine wines.

Of course, there'd be no mention of wife or kids, because Drake Hogan would die a professional bachelor.

His heart twisted a little.

"Son!" Gramps demanded, bursting Drake's fantasy. "Give a hand."

Bent over the headstone, Gramps's huge shadowy body, topped with a head of electrified hair, was a ghoulish presence. Drake shuddered. His buddy Russell thought *he'd* lived through a few tense moments with a Harley dude his wife knew. Russell's fears were trivial compared to Drake's current reality, where he starred in a backyard cemetery story that gave the word *plot* a whole new twist.

"Son, have you gone deaf?" Gramps unrolled his massive form, effectively blocking out a major chunk of the horizon. In the descending night shadows, his huge body resembled a monster.

Drake's gaze darted down.

An oversized monster wearing an apron. As if the Cookie Monster had been hanging out near a nuclear plant too long.

"Son?" The Cookie Monster lurched forward.

Drake's dark-edged fantasy popped. "No Suzie, No Drake." *That* was lingo they'd understand. He eased one foot back along the cement. Freedom was a mere dash to the kitchen door, through the house and out the crazy eggplant purple door to his sane red Sylvia.

"We just need to carry Suzie out to the car," LuLu said apologetically, holding open her hands as though she had nothing to hide. "Then you can drop off the three of us and we'll be out of your life forever."

His gaze traveled up her long, tanned legs, over the quirky outfit, to those brown eyes. She had a way of looking at him that jumbled his thoughts. Face it, she was sexy, cute. And he didn't like the idea of her being out of his life forever.

On the other hand, they talk about that chunk of rock as though it's a human being.

Would they talk about him that way? "How about if the four of us barbecue tonight?" *Four. LuLu, Babaloo, Suzie and Drake.* He silently vowed to never again refer to a date as "deadweight."

Although his foot felt more like a doorstop than an appendage, Drake slid back another step, hoping he wouldn't accidentally land in one of the decorative cacti. An ankle speared with needles would hinder his escape. "My car isn't, uh, equipped to carry someone—something—that heavy."

Gramps grunted. "She doesn't weigh that much."

Drake fumbled behind him. The screen door had to be near. "Don't you two have a car? Or a hearse?"

"Here, Gramps, let me help." LuLu crossed to the headstone. Firing a look in Drake's direction, she muttered, "No, we've never had a car. Or a *hearse*." She gave her curly head a disbelieving shake. "Gramps and I have bikes. Plus I'm the queen of mass transit.'

As Cookie Monster and his granddaughter adjusted their hold on Suzie, Drake saw his chance. He spun on his heel, ready to exit stage left and leave this B horror flick.

He gripped the door handle and yanked open the screen door.

A loud sniff halted his grand escape.

A loud, sad and very feminine sniff.

"Drake," LuLu said, her voice soft and frightened. "We need your help. Just this one favor and we'll be out of your life forever. I promise." From overhead, an owl hooted, as though echoing her vow.

Drake was all too familiar with the ache in a girl's voice when she was at her wit's end. Add to that a sniff and a tear and Big Brother was ready to save the day.

He played with the door handle.

"I promise," she repeated, her words barely breaking a whisper.

Her hopelessness tore at Drake's gut. Mainly because he knew she wasn't weak. He had the sense that it took every shred of her self-esteem to ask for his, or anyone's, help.

"No Suzie, no Babaloo," Gramps added, obviously tunnel-visioned to his own needs.

Drake released the door, which slapped against the doorjamb several times before finally stopping. "Enough with the no-no's." He turned around, ready to face the woman for whom he was willing to play knight in shining armor.

LuLu stood half in the spill of kitchen light, half in the dark. Even five feet away, he caught a glistening tear in her eye. Her shoulder slumped, as though she couldn't bear the burden any longer. He'd seen hundreds of acting students practice long hours to show hurt, betrayal, grief. But for LuLu, this was no act. Her soul was bare, her pain exposed.

For a crazy moment, he had the irrational urge to take her in his arms and comfort her. She might be spunky and head-strong, but right now she was vulnerable. And needy. And she had every right to be—two thugs were hot on her trail and he was wasting precious moments with his reticence.

He clapped his hands together, more to break the mood than to show exuberance. Something scurried across the surrounding gravel. "Let's shove—uh, carry—Suzie to the 'Vette and put an end to this nonsense before we all need headstones."

Staggering and huffing, the three of them carried the slab of stone, on top of which was balanced Gramps's duffel and LuLu's workout bags, to the car. Suzie and the bags barely fit into the opened trunk. Gramps tried to force the lid closed, the result being a grating sound following by a crack. As Drake corralled Gramps and LuLu into the passenger seat, he tried not to dwell on what sounded like a broken hinge—or the permanent dent Suzie was undoubtedly carving into Sylvia's trunk lid.

Oblivious to Drake's concerns, LuLu settled onto Gramps's lap in the passenger seat. With no back seat, she either had to sit there or they'd have to strap her over the hood. Not that the idea didn't give Drake a moment of perverse pleasure. If he hadn't known this woman's name before, he did now: Trouble.

He jumped into the driver's seat, slammed his door and twisted the ignition key. "Where to?" he asked over the rev-ving engine.

LuLu scrunched her face. "One of the motels off the Strip."

The 'Vette chugged down the street, its pace sluggish. It was that damn weight in the back, thought Drake glumly. His svelte Sylvia had been on a binge. Like a beautiful woman who'd consumed an extra-large pepperoni pizza, Sylvia wasn't gonna be dancing lightly tonight.

Drake slowly drove for several blocks, took a left and pulled over to the curb. It was safe to stop here, on an anonymous side street with no overhead lights.

Cutting the engine, he asked, "Why stay here?" He turned to look at his passengers. "Let's drive to another town where you won't be hounded by those goons." It would be a slow drive, but they'd be safer away from Vegas.

In a trace of moonlight, he thought he caught a look of anxiousness on LuLu's face. "I take my reflexology exam in the morning. I've waited six months for this exam, and if I don't take it tomorrow, I have to wait another six months. I have no choice—we have to stay in town."

"Reflexology?" Drake asked.

"In laymen's terms, foot massage," LuLu explained. "I have a great job offer that starts in two weeks if I pass this exam. Once-in-a-lifetime offer. Great pay. But best of all, the golden opportunity to escape Grave."

"Grave?" This family needed to get out more. This cemetery fetish was being taken a little far. Then it hit him. This was the king thug who commandeered the other thugs. "Does he have a last name? And please, don't tell me that people really dig him."

The joke slipped by unnoticed. "Grave Murray," LuLu answered. "He runs Capri, a casino. I was a makeup artist there."

"He's a bum," Gramps grumbled. "That's what's wrong with the world today—too many bums."

"If he's such a bum, why'd you continue working there?" Drake was glad he couldn't catch the full look on LuLu's shadowed face. In the following silence, he got the distinct impression he'd trotted onto a sensitive subject.

"Paid better than similar jobs, which weren't exactly in abundance. And I needed the money to help support…" Her voice trailed off, but Drake could have finished the sentence. She supported her grandfather. She might look and act quirky, but she had her feet planted firmly in reality. Being the family breadwinner, she had no choice.

Meanwhile, she was working hard to develop a new career. And Drake knew what that took. Daily perseverance. Something he related to because he'd spent years saving money so he could return to graduate school and get his doctorate in child psychology.

He rubbed a knot in his neck as he stared overhead at the twinkling stars, which glittered like the rhinestones on LuLu's shoes. In a funny way, it made sense that a woman who wore rhinestone-studded shoes would want a profession involving feet.

He dropped his hand to the shift knob and looked back down at LuLu and Gramps. "Okay," he said with resignation. "We find a hotel room for tonight. Tomorrow, after the exam, you two take a bus to another town."

"Nope." LuLu responded firmly with a shake of her head. "I have to go into the hospital after the exam."

Drake nodded as though everything was perfectly clear in a muddy sort of way. "But I thought by marrying me, you escaped marrying the guy who was forcing you to have some operation. No marriage, no operation, right?" Not that he understood what *this* was all about.

LuLu sighed. "I accidentally swallowed…something…so I need the operation. Doctor says I have three, maybe four days before it's…crucial. I just didn't want to go under the knife with Grave controlling things—I feared I'd never wake up."

"Accidentally swallowed?" Gramps asked. "Cupcake, what is it?"

So that's what this was all about. Drake gave Cupcake a once-over. With that funky layered outfit, she could have swallowed anything and it wouldn't show. "Is it larger than a bread box?"

Even in the faint moonlight, he caught her give-me-a-break look. "Smaller. A diamond."

Drake waited a beat before responding. "Should I ask why?"

"Long story."

"No doubt."

"I licked it."

After another beat, Drake said, "That's a short story."

"Grave wanted me to transport some diamonds to another state, one of his 'deals.' The way some people are addicted to booze or drugs, Grave is addicted to gambling and deals. Anyway, if I did this diamond deal, which he needed done by noon tomorrow, he promised to cut Gramps's gambling debt in half. I didn't want to do anything illegal. I was stalling. When Grave left the room, I was looking at the diamonds and—"

"You're right," Drake said, tapping his fingers lightly on the shift knob. "This is a long story."

Gramps, obviously mesmerized by the tale, leaned his huge face close to LuLu. "You were looking at the diamonds, and...?"

She sighed heavily. "I picked one up and held it to the light. It was reddish. Beautiful. I wanted to see how it sparkled, so I licked it."

After a moment of silence, Drake said, "Licking is not swallowing."

"Grave surprised me. I jumped. So did the diamond—down my throat. I swallowed. At first Grave thought about taking me to his doctor and having my stomach pumped, but then he figured it was simpler to keep me in his office, feed me fiber and wait for the diamond to—"

"I get the picture," interrupted Drake.

"Anyway," LuLu continued, "when the fiber didn't do the trick, Grave decided to take me to his doctor and have X rays taken. That's when it was discovered that the diamond was stuck at the opening to my appendix. But I refused to have the operation—I mean, who in their right mind would want Grave's doctor poking around in their insides? Anyway, Grave decided that if he was my husband, he could force the operation, so he had his goons whisk me away to a chapel. I escaped. I married you. Now the three of us are here. End of story." She cast a look at Drake. "And it wasn't so long, either."

"So in a sense," Drake said, "*I'm* now a diamond smuggler." He made an exasperated sound. "Grave might be addicted to gambling, but I detest the sport."

"Sorry," LuLu murmured. "Sorry about your trunk, too. You've gone out of your way for two strangers. You're a saint."

Sainthood took a second seat to the broken trunk. *My beautiful Sylvia, damaged by these cemetery groupies.* Drake squeezed hard on the wooden shift knob. He didn't mind being their rescuer—he'd spent years honing that talent with his sisters—but for the first time in his life, playing knight in shining armor hurt the only thing he'd ever given himself: Sylvia. Not only had she cost him two years' income-tax returns plus a five-year loan, he'd babied and buffed her every weekend for the past six years. His relationship with Sylvia was the longest and most loving he'd ever had.

And in one night, she was forever ruined.

"What's wrong?" LuLu asked quietly.

"Nothing," he mumbled.

"Gotta flow?" Gramps asked.

"No." Drake shot him a dark look.

"It's Suzie, isn't it?" LuLu asked.

"It's just that…she's scattering granite flakes and denting Sylvia's trunk. Plus I have you two straining the leather upholstery—custom ordered, by the way." He glared at LuLu. Through gritted teeth he asked, "Do you know how expensive it is to reupholster a car like this?"

"Do you know how expensive I am with this diamond wedged in my appendix?" she retorted in an equally edgy tone. "Let's get a little perspective here."

Drake stared at her stomach. "How—"

"How expensive?" Gramps interrupted, finishing Drake's thought.

LuLu looked from one to the other. "Forty grand," she finally said. "Give or take."

"Forty?" Gramps slapped the door. "Cupcake, I know you hide money from me all the time, but this is taking it a little far."

"Speaking of far, let's get going." Drake turned the ignition key. Shifting into first, he muttered, "This is the worst blind date I've ever been on."

LuLu folded her arms over her chest. "This is *not* a date. Just because we got married doesn't make this a date."

Easing his foot down on the gas pedal, Drake wished he hadn't used his last toothpick earlier. He desperately needed something to chomp on. "You're right," he said tightly. "We smashed into each other, ran into the chapel and got married even though we didn't even know each other's real name. That hardly qualifies as a *date*." The car rolled forward. "Thanks for the reality check. I was beginning to question my sanity."

"You kids got married?" Gramps asked, his voice filled with hurt. "Without telling Suzie and me first?"

"We meant to tell you two," Drake answered, shifting gears, "but we got overwhelmed with passion and just couldn't stop ourselves. But we want to tell you everything. Let's plan a double date—you, Suzie, LuLu and me—and catch up on the particulars."

LuLu aimed a small kick at Drake's leg. "Another long story, Babaloo. We sort of got married, but not really. We pretended so I could escape Grave's thugs. But it's handy they *think* we're married because now Grave won't pressure me to marry him."

Gramps grunted. "Never liked Grave. Only sissy boys dye their hair."

Dye. Drake shuddered at the play on words.

"We've talked about this before, Babaloo. Grave has naturally jet black hair."

"Naturally," Gramps repeated, obviously not convinced. "If you ask me, Grave is a bottle Elvis."

Not only did they have a thing for cemeteries, Drake thought, but for colors too, it seemed. No doubt that eggplant purple paint was custom mixed.

"This guy seems better," Gramps continued, patting Drake roughly on the arm. "After that flow problem is taken care of, he'll be in good shape."

"I don't have a flow prob—"

"Can't believe you kids kept your marriage a secret," interrupted Gramps.

Drake wondered if Gramps intentionally cut him off or spoke his mind no matter who was talking.

"Times were simpler when Suzie and I got married," Gramps continued. "We just fell in love and got married. That's what's wrong with the world today—everything's gotta be complicated. People get married with diamonds in their guts instead of on their fingers, with gangsters forcing them out of their homes, escaping in fancy cars with girl names."

Although he could have done without the girl-name comment, Drake had to agree. He reflected how life was definitely more complicated than he'd like. Which was one major reason he'd successfully avoided matrimony—well, until today. He liked his simple bachelor's life, where he answered to no one. Nobody to complain if he left socks on the floor. Nobody to answer to if he wanted a night out with the boys. A no-muss, no-fuss life-style where he occasionally enjoyed a beautiful woman's company with no strings attached.

He glanced over at LuLu and Gramps. From the way she was sitting in his lap, her arm draped comfortably around her grandfather's broad shoulders, Drake could see that they belonged together. They had obviously faced a lot and were willing to weather this latest setback as well, because they were committed to each other.

Committed.

A shooting star cut a fiery path through the sky. Watching its blazing path disappear into the heavens, Drake experienced a twinge of regret. He'd never know what it was like to be committed. To be truly in love.

Commitment. Inhaling the dry desert air, he wished it would blow the word out of his mind. But it stayed, coiling through his thoughts. *Commitment.* He didn't regret how he lived. He had the best of both worlds: love without shackles. Any man in his right mind would envy Drake's professional-bachelor life-style.

But the justification felt hollow.

A few minutes later, they turned onto Las Vegas Boulevard.

He stepped on the gas and merged with the traffic. LuLu tapped Drake on the shoulder. When he looked over, she held up her thumb and forefinger in a "small amount" gesture. "Don't go far," she mouthed.

He eased to a stop at a red light. Not going far made sense. He remembered from past trips how sluggish traffic got farther down the Strip. It would be crazy to be stuck in slow-moving traffic with a huge, pink marble slab hanging out of his trunk and LuLu and Gramps stacked on top of each other in the front seat like human poker chips. Might as well hang a sign on the car saying, Here We Are, Thugs!

"There they are!" yelled a baritone voice.

Cold dread washed over Drake. He looked to his left. In the lane next to him was a gold Chevy—and the Blues Brothers.

The short one, in the driver's seat, leaned forward and glared at them. In the reflection from streetlights, Drake could make out his chipmunk cheeks, which looked even more puffed out. His cohort pointed at them through the open passenger window, a look of stupefaction on his face.

"Pull over," the short one yelled at Drake.

"Yeah," echoed the tall one, looking confused as to why.

Drake wondered if anybody was ever home in the tall one's head.

"Oh my God, don't pull over!" LuLu cried, clutching Drake's arm.

The light was still red. Drake slid LuLu a do-I-look-stupid? look. With his head turned away from the Chevy, he glanced at the cross traffic from the right. One lone car approached; it wouldn't enter the intersection soon. "Any cars coming the other way?" he asked quietly, wriggling his eyebrows toward the left.

Gramps and LuLu leaned forward and back. LuLu, obviously aware she was being scrutinized by the thugs, barely opened her lips to say no.

Drake slammed his foot on the gas and prayed Sylvia's pepperoni gut wouldn't slow down their grand move.

3

LuLu SHRIEKED. The Corvette chugged, jumped and died. Muttering an expletive, Drake pumped the gas and turned the ignition key. They were smack in the middle of an intersection with an ominous red light overhead. And he thought the tall Blues Brother looked stupid? Drake's middle-of-the-intersection breakdown made Tall Blues look like the president of Mensa.

Brakes squealed. In his peripheral vision, Drake caught the blur of a skidding car. The air reeked of burning rubber. Through the driver's window, a burly hand flashed a one-fingered salute.

"Hurry!" LuLu screamed, clutching Drake's shoulder. "Here comes another one!"

Another one? "One" could be anything from another burly hand to another skidding car. With a frantic twist of the key, Drake stomped on the gas. Sylvia, despite her pepperoni binge, leaped forward. From the right, a van swerved to avoid them, its horn blasting. A barrage of expletives peppered the air.

And then, with a miraculous burst of speed, Sylvia charged through the intersection. As they sailed past the far crosswalk, Drake had a fleeting image of Sylvia as a sassy victor reaching the finish line.

But this was hardly finished. Drake glanced in his rearview mirror. The gold Chevy, with a head emerging from either side, still sat at the red light.

"That was a hell of a move, son," Gramps yelled as they sped down the Strip. "You can fight alongside me anytime."

Drake flicked a drip of sweat from his hairline. "Fight?"

LuLu leaned close to Drake's ear. Her words competing

with the rush of air, she yelled, "Gramps is an ex-marine. He means you were really something." Leaning back, she patted Drake's arm in congratulations.

It was the first time her touch hadn't been a clutch or a grip. If it took near death to bring out LuLu's compassion, no wonder Suzie-the-Headstone was doted over.

"We all were almost *ex*-somethings," Drake muttered. "Ex-human beings." Ahead, a pyramid rose into the sky, its point a sharp outline against the hazy glow of city lights. Only in Vegas did they build monstrous hotel complexes that resembled one of the seven wonders of the world.

And they'd be the eighth if he didn't lose the Blues Brothers.

He gritted his teeth, fighting a surge of irritation. What in the hell was he doing racing down the Strip with gangsters hot on his tail? God, he missed his L.A. bachelor pad, where the essence of life was sipping Chablis while listening to Billie Holliday. And, if circumstances were right, having a babe on his lap.

He looked over at LuLu, her mass of curls uncoiling wildly in the wind. And Gramps, his mane of white hair shooting straight out behind him like an unraveled cotton ball.

Hardly the kind of babes with whom Drake typically kept company.

"People," he said, raising his voice to the baritone boom that kept students in line. "That light back there is going to turn green any moment. Madonna will be closing in. Let's get off this main drag."

With a quick glance over his shoulder, he shot across two lanes and took a sharp right. After several blocks, he swung right again down a narrow side street.

"Look for a place where we can park and not be seen from the road," he yelled.

This part of Vegas obviously wasn't a tourist favorite. Along a buckled stretch of sidewalk were a few bail-bond businesses, a laundromat and a liquor store. Other than the man leaving the latter clutching a box of wine, the only other signs of life were some bedraggled palm trees.

I'll hunt down a phone booth, look up a nearby motel, get them set up and split.

Drake smiled. Chablis and Billie would be his tonight.

"Bingo!" LuLu squealed, pointing at an oversize thunderbolt outlined in yellow lights over the name Thor's Hideaway. The neon bolt blinked on and off like a gaudy beacon.

"Looks like a strip joint," Drake shouted.

"It's a motel joint!" LuLu grabbed the steering wheel. "Turn here!"

Fighting for control of the car, Drake swore as Sylvia swerved abruptly. The car bumped over a curb, then rattled and shuddered as they veered down the sidewalk toward the neon thunderbolt. As his and LuLu's hands battled for dominance, Sylvia's front fender caromed off a trash can, which sprang away in a wide arc before clanging into oblivion.

Drake tightened his hold on the wheel, cursing loudly.

Gramps was bellowing something about Iwo Jima.

LuLu was yelling, too, but Drake's expletives drowned out hers.

Guiding the car with his left hand, Drake shoved LuLu away with his right. In control of Sylvia once again, he forced the car off the sidewalk and down an alley, where, after spinning in a ninety-degree turn, he careened into a parking lot and slammed on the brakes.

The following moments of silence were punctuated by heavy breathing as the three of them heaved and gulped deep breaths. Drake hadn't been this spent by a ride since he was thirteen and the Tilt-A-Whirl ride at the county fair spun amok for thirty minutes. His cousin Andy had thrown up the rest of the night. It had been a sign of fledging manhood that Drake had managed to keep down three corn dogs and a cotton candy. Not an easy feat, but a necessary rite of passage.

Another necessary rite of passage, at this very moment, was to stop himself from saying things he knew he'd regret. Things about crazy women in sci-fi outfits grabbing the steering wheel of a moving car. Maybe LuLu didn't own a car, but she sure as hell thought she had squatter's rights to another's vehicle.

Rolling his tongue against the inside of his cheek, he stared her down. There wasn't much light in this parking lot, but even in the feeble glow from an overhead lamp, he saw her big brown eyes widen in alarm.

She brushed a curl out of her face. "You're mad," she said matter-of-factly.

"No," he said calmly, finding his voice, "I'm thrilled that you almost killed us."

"I took control—otherwise you would have driven past Thor's Hideaway."

"I wasn't going to drive past. And if I *was* going to drive past, I would have driven on the *street*."

He balled his hands into tight fists. Otherwise he might throttle her. As though explaining the situation to a child, he continued, "Streets are for cars. Sidewalks are for people. By driving on the sidewalk, we might have run over one of those people. And I, being in the driver's seat, would have been arrested for manslaughter." Marriage, gangsters, headstones, manslaughter. He didn't need to teach drama anymore. He *lived* it.

She straightened and pulled her shoulders back. "You just don't like a woman taking control."

He wouldn't touch that one with a ten-foot pool stick. He unballed his hands and flexed his fingers. "No, I just don't like a woman—or anyone else—invading my steering space."

A look of hurt nobility filled LuLu's eyes—a look he'd seen his sisters pull many times. He held on to his fury, determined not to succumb to any feminine wiles.

As though through telepathy, she seemed to read his mind. Her wide-eyed gaze narrowed. They stared at each other, the moments stretching into a long, uncomfortable minute.

"Hey, you two lovebirds," Gramps interrupted, sounding falsely chipper, "it's your wedding night. This is no time to fight." He patted LuLu's arm with one hand while roughly nudging Drake with the other, as if to say, "Make up with your bride."

"We're not lovebirds," LuLu answered coolly, never breaking eye contact with Drake.

"No, just man and wife," Drake responded tersely.

"Man and *woman*," she corrected.

"Or, in our case, man and *hardhead*."

"That's enough, you two!" Gramps shifted in his seat. "LuLu, I'm tired of being your platform while you argue. Get off, Cupcake. Time to check in before your old Gramps checks out."

Breaking her staring match with Drake, she opened the passenger door and said sweetly to her grandfather, "Now, Babaloo, don't start that checking-out stuff again. You're going to live a long time."

He grunted as she slid off his lap. "Long enough to finish Suzie's headstone. Then, Gabriel, blow your horn, 'cause it's the pearly gates for this old soldier." Gramps rubbed his legs before stepping out of the car to join his granddaughter.

They stood facing each other, their silhouettes outlined against several electric beer signs in the back window of a convenience store that bordered the parking lot. Spontaneously, LuLu reached up and hugged her grandfather.

Drake watched in silence. Despite all the acting he'd taught, he'd never witnessed such a simple act of devotion. Had he ever held a loved one in such an embrace? He thought back to his sisters or his mom. Sometimes they shared a quick hug, but never a lingering, loving one. He hadn't shared such a moment with a girlfriend, either.

A lump rose in his throat. He looked away, embarrassed—and surprised—by the unexpected well of emotion. Absently, he rubbed at the stubble on his chin and watched a bird flit quietly through the night sky and land on a telephone wire. The solitary creature cocked its head and seemed to eye warily the act of familial love below.

Was that his destiny? To be alone, observing others, never experiencing true love?

When Drake looked back, LuLu and Gramps were breaking their embrace.

"You sure Thor's Hideaway is a motel?" Drake asked, gesturing toward the flashing yellow thunderbolt that hung in the sky a half block away. Mainly he spoke to break the mood.

And to distance himself from his emotions. "After this wild day, the last thing we need is to stumble into a strip joint."

Gramps stopped midstretch and jerked his gaze to Drake. "Time to learn rule number one, son—trust your wife. If she says it's a motel, it's a motel. You'll save yourself a lot of grief over the years if you learn this simple rule up front."

Sighing audibly, LuLu dragged her hand through her mass of windblown curls. "It's a motel, okay? Trust me because I know this town, not because you happened to marry me."

Stepping out of the car, Drake checked out the immediate area. The overhead lamp, nailed onto the side of a telephone pole, cast a faint blue-white glow over the parking lot. Clumps of grass sprouted through cracks in the asphalt. To their right was the tacky convenience store, serving a noble purpose—it prevented their being seen from the main street. An astute thug would have to follow a maze to find them here.

Short Blues, the astute one, obviously hadn't done that.

Tall Blues, the non-astute one, lived in a permanent maze.

Which meant LuLu and Gramps were safe. For the time being.

Drake shifted his gaze to Gramps, who was raising his legs in some sort of bizarre calisthenics. His lifting and kicking while wearing that frilly white apron nearly destroyed every cheerleader fantasy Drake had ever had.

Drake headed toward the alley. "You two—uh, three—stay here. I'll go to Thor's and see if they have a room. Be back in a few."

"THAT YOUNG MAN'S GOT the makings of a good husband," LuLu's grandfather said, watching Drake's exiting form.

Husband? LuLu poked the toe of her rhinestone sneaker at a crack in the asphalt, wondering how to discuss the truth of the situation with Gramps. He still hoped LuLu would fall in love and raise a family, despite her adamant denials that she'd ever marry. She'd grown up basically alone because her own parents were always on the road. The only families she witnessed were those on TV shows, like the *Andy Griffith Show*, her favorite. When Gramps and Suzie moved in, she'd thought her life had magically become Mayberry—Suzie was Aunt Bee, Gramps was Pa and she was Opie. A happy threesome.

"Yes, sir, a fine husband," Gramps continued, stretching his arms over his head.

She stopped running her toe along the crack in the asphalt. "I'm going to give it to you straight. I'm married to that guy, but he's not my husband. I mean, we had a wedding ceremony, but in name only. Not *our* names, though. The minister thinks he's Rudolpho. But he's not."

Gramps ruffled his fingers through his hair and squinted at something in the distance. "The minister's named Rudolpho?"

"No. The minister thinks my husband's—I mean, that guy's—name is Rudolpho."

"I thought you called him Drake." Gramps looked back at her. "So what does he do for a living? Have you met his family? Have you thought about…having your own family?" Gramps grinned, his face scrunching into a sea of wrinkles.

Yes, but not with a husband attached. They'd had this conversation many times before, and she didn't want to repeat it now. Gramps had his heart set on her having a happy marriage, the kind he and Suzie had had. But even if LuLu *did* want a spouse, Drake Hogan was marriage material like silk was seat upholstery material. She glared at the Corvette, imagining the stories Sylvia could tell. That car wasn't just a motor vehicle, it was a date machine.

Just like its owner, no doubt. "Don't get your hopes up, Babaloo. Drake's a prima donna lover boy who thinks he's Wayne Newton incarnate."

Squeezing his chin with his thumb and forefinger, Gramps spent the next few minutes pacing and thinking. "Wayne Newton dyes his hair black, too," he finally said. "Just like Grave." He nodded sagely. "That's your problem, Cupcake. You're mad at all men because of Grave. And you know I'm not handing you propeller wash."

It was his World War II euphemism for bull. "No, Gramps, you're being honest."

"That's right, Cupcake. I just want you to have a good life.

To have the love of a good man.'' His voice, often so gruff, now sounded as though it had been dipped in sugar. It took this tone whenever he spoke from his heart.

"I'll have a good life," LuLu conceded. But she left off the part about the love of a good man. Frankly, she didn't believe it was possible. Once upon a time she had, with Grave, but not since.

As though reading her mind, Gramps nodded sagely. "I remember Grave as a kid. Tough, but he had heart. He got tougher, though, as he grew older. Let greed corrupt him, Cupcake. He gambled with more than money. He gambled his integrity. And lost."

Grave's deceit still shook her emotionally. They'd grown up on the same block. As a kid, she remembered watching Grave through the living room window as he played with his brothers. Grave was the youngest of three boys, but definitely the most insolent. More than once she'd seen him goad one of his brothers into a fight, which ended with the brother in a headlock, agreeing to give Grave some toy or money in exchange for freedom.

After her parents died and her grandparents moved in, Grave showed up at her door and asked if she'd like to go bike riding. She knew his parents had put him up to it—probably his punishment for some stunt he'd pulled at home—but the parental discipline had backfired. Grave started liking the visits to her home, which seemed to coincide with mealtimes. Gramps's years as a short-order cook, combined with his obsession for putting chocolate sauce on almost everything, made his meals a treat for kids.

Years later, after her grandmother had died and Grave had become the pit boss at Capri, he'd hired LuLu—at a good salary—to be the wardrobe mistress for the showgirls. Just as when she'd been a little girl and Grave had shown up to ask her to play, he now showed up as an adult to offer help. Money was tight at home. Her grandfather was too old to find employment. The job meant she and Gramps could make ends meet.

Working at Capri, she'd overhear people talking about

Grave's bullying tactics and illegal activities, but had decided to ignore the gossip. He'd helped her make a living, and she owed him her loyalty. Eventually her loyalty evolved into a crush. Before she knew it, she and Grave were embroiled in an affair, her first big romance. If other people wore their hearts on their sleeves, she wore it as an entire outfit. Her previous plans to never marry now seemed like distant childish fears.

But it grew increasingly difficult to ignore Grave's duplicity. As his power grew, so did his ego. By the time he became part owner of Capri, he felt entitled to act out criminal schemes and act on sexual urges. She'd been oblivious of his two-timing until the afternoon she'd walked into his office and discovered him on the couch with a big blonde, who'd tried to explain their activity as "artificial perspiration." At the time, LuLu hadn't known whether to laugh or cry. But she did plenty of the latter over the following months.

"True, Gramps," she agreed. "People can gamble away their integrity."

"Doesn't mean all men are meatballs."

"I never said that." No, but she certainly acted like she believed it. Oh, there'd been the occasional date, but she always had a reason why she didn't want to bother with more. After Grave, she didn't want another man to get close, because trusting love meant chancing pain. All the more reason to forgo the traditional family unit and adopt her own child. LuLu, baby and Gramps. Just like LuLu, Suzie and Gramps. Three people could lead a very happy life.

Gramps scratched his chin. "Well, you landed yourself a pretty good man with that Drake—or Rudolpho—fellow." He gestured to the car. "Looks as though he makes a decent living. He helped us escape those thugs, which shows he has plenty of courage. And he obviously cares for my granddaughter, which shows he has smarts. Yep, he's a lollapalooza." Gramps harrumphed under his breath. "Although, in the future, I hope he waits for lights to turn green before charging through intersections."

Drake's voice broke in. "Advice taken. And what's a lol-lapalooza?"

"Means you're grade A, son."

Drake cocked his head toward LuLu. "See? I'm not such a bad guy, you know."

No, he wasn't. He was a rather good one, in fact. If he hadn't entered their lives, she'd probably be under the knife right now. And Gramps? No doubt Grave would have hunted him down—possibly threatened to do him harm if LuLu didn't sign over the house to repay Gramps's debt.

"Hey, don't dwell on it," murmured Drake, interrupting her thoughts. He had to be reacting to the look of fear on her face, for his tone had softened. "I was glad to help."

For a long moment, their gazes held. Just as they had back at the chapel, right after being pronounced husband and wife. She remembered how his blue eyes had deepened to indigo right before he'd kissed her.

And that kiss…

Warm.

Inviting.

Hardly the kiss of a man doing her a favor.

Her insides fluttered with heat. The unexpected reaction pleasantly surprised her. And at the same time, jolted loose an old, painful memory of what it had been like to fall in love.

Drake cleared his throat. "Yes, well, here's the room key." He held up a key with what looked to be a miniature thunderbolt attached. "Venus. Last room they had available." Looking at the key, he shrugged. "Guess Venus and Thor knew each other way back when." He swung the key around his finger. "Okay, let's get this show on the road."

"Kids, I've been thinking," Gramps said, his voice so loud LuLu was certain everyone in the convenience store could hear. "It's your wedding night. Take the room. I'll put Suzie near the bushes and sleep here, next to her—"

"Babaloo—" LuLu interrupted.

"Son," Gramps said, overriding her, "help my grand-daughter to your room, then bring me a blanket and pillow. I roughed it in the South Pacific, I can rough it in this parking lot.''

"No way, Gramps." LuLu said. "You and *I* will stay in the motel room. Just in case we have to get out fast, we'll leave Suzie in the parking lot where we can pick her up later.'' LuLu looked around, then gestured toward the bushes clustered at the edge of the convenience store. "We'll put her behind those bushes. She'll be safe there.''

Gramps, his massive head bent, stared at the bushes as though they were the enemy. Trying to cover the emotion in his voice, he said, "She's never been alone." He pointed accusingly at the store. "And I don't like her being under those beer signs. My Suzie has class.''

LuLu looked at the electric signs, each brand name brightly outlined in neon oranges and yellows. One sign, which flickered as though on its last watt, hung at a drunken angle. She had to agree. Suzie would never have hung out near such signs. A champagne advertisement, yes. A beer slogan, no. Still, it was best to leave Suzie here.

"No one will sneak into this out-of-the-way parking lot and beat the bushes for a pink marble headstone,'' she reasoned sweetly.

Gramps gave a disgruntled snort.

"Plus," Drake added, "the culprits would undoubtedly want the letters on the headstone aligned, not crooked.''

LuLu bit her bottom lip. That headstone was her Gramps's masterpiece. Drake would have hurt him less with a loaded gun.

She slid a look at her grandfather.

He stood stiffly, his attention riveted on Drake. His unruly mass of white hair, eerily highlighted by the overhead lamp, stood on end, giving him the appearance of a deranged dandelion. "I haven't left Suzie alone *once* in the past seven years.''

He strode to the Corvette trunk and placed his hand gingerly on the marble slab. He stroked it lovingly. "I could see her out my bedroom window at any hour of the day or night. She was never alone. Were you, baby? You were never alone.''

On the second "alone," Gramps's voice cracked. Looking away, he swiped at the corner of his eye.

Drake shook his head as though wishing he could erase the gaff. "Sir—"

"When *we're* alone," Gramps said, cutting him off, "we'll have a man-to-man talk about how the letters are artistically arranged, not crooked." He turned away and busied himself with removing his duffel bag.

In the following silence, a breeze sifted through the parking lot, carrying with it the scent of jasmine. Sweet, light, just like her grandmother Suzie had been. Time for LuLu to be the same. "Babaloo," she said softly, "Suzie isn't sleeping in this parking lot and neither are you. We'll take her to the room."

After a brief hesitation, Gramps nodded his assent.

As he returned his bag to the trunk, LuLu crossed back to Drake. "Watch those "crooked" comments, okay?" she whispered.

In the dim light, she caught a surprised look in his eyes. "Sorry."

A guy admitting he was wrong? This was one for the Guinness records.

Drake touched her arm. "I should have thought before speaking."

The heat of his hand against her skin made it difficult to focus on the conversation. She fought the constriction in her throat as she spoke. "Before you leave tonight, make a bit of a fuss over Suzie." If any guy knew how to do that, it had to be Drake Hogan. She glanced over at Gramps, who was pre-occupied with dusting off the headstone.

When she looked back, Drake had moved closer. "What should I compliment her on?"

He stood so near that LuLu swore she could see small reflections of light within his blue eyes, which looked deeply into her own. If before she had trouble focusing on their conversation, the intensity of his stare made her nearly forget what they were discussing. Worse, he hadn't moved his hand. His touch now felt like fire. When she spoke, her words came out breathy, as though she'd forgotten how to fill her lungs with air.

"You're asking *me* how to compliment a woman? Isn't that like asking Bill Murray to give Jean-Claude Van Damme kick boxing lessons?"

One side of Drake's mouth curled upward. His sexy grin was lethal enough to be labeled a killer smile. "Okay," he said huskily. "How about if I compliment her on her eyes?"

His breath warmed her neck. Small currents of electricity skittered down her spine. "Her eyes?" LuLu said hoarsely, realizing the best she could do at this point was stupidly repeat his words and fake the rest. "You never saw her eyes."

Drake was so near she could smell his cologne. It was musky. *Dangerous.* She closed her eyes and inhaled deeply.

"Her lips?" Drake asked.

LuLu pursed hers, recalling their kiss after being pronounced man and wife. She felt momentarily dizzy reliving the heady sensation of his lips against her mouth. "You never...saw her lips, either."

Drake toyed with one of LuLu's curls. "Then I'll have to compliment her on her hair...its silky texture, its sweet scent...."

"You smell good, too."

LuLu's eyes popped open. "I mean you—you...feel good." She squeezed shut her eyes again, wishing one of the cracks in the asphalt would open up and swallow her whole. "Fell," she corrected quickly, trying to sound adult and mature and knowing she was failing miserably at both. She cleared her throat. "You know, when we fell on the sidewalk."

"I know what you mean." His voice had dropped to a velvet murmur. "Let's get to the motel room so you can fall into bed."

Motel room.

Images of rumpled sheets, musky cologne and Drake's naked, muscular body infused every single brain cell. She reeled backward, away from his touch, his scent, his confidence. The last thing she needed was to *fall*—fall for Drake Hogan. Small technicality that he was her husband. She barely knew the guy.

"Right," she said, taking another step back. This man didn't turn women into putty, he transformed them into pulp. She clapped her hands together. "Let's get this road on the show." Stumbling toward the Corvette, she realized it would take more than one hand clap to shake her Drake-induced trance.

During the next few minutes, the three of them drove down the alley and into the Thor's Hideaway parking lot. After carrying their cargo into the room and setting it on the faded, pumpkin-colored carpet, Gramps straightened and looked around. "Looks more like Thor's laundry room than Thor's Hideaway."

LuLu stepped gingerly over a pile of sheets on the floor. It also looked like her room at home. Her free time was spent riding her bike or seeing action-adventure flicks. Washing and tidying were low on her priority list. Gramps, however, believed cleanliness reflected one's character. He might be loose with money, but he was tight with household duties.

Muttering under his breath, Gramps picked up a wad of sheets next to one of the queen-size beds. "What is this place—a do-it-yourself motel room?" He looked around. "Suzie has never been in such a mess. I always kept our bedroom shoe-shine bright."

LuLu flashed Drake a meaningful look. "Shoe-shine bright means very, very clean."

"So I gathered."

"Clean enough to see your reflection in your shoes," Gramps added, scanning the room. "Where are fresh sheets?"

Drake motioned toward two battered-looking wooden doors. "Front desk said they'd be in the closet." He shrugged. "Sorry about the mess. The woman at the desk said they wouldn't be getting maid service until tomorrow, but this was the last room, so I took it anyway. Better than having the three of us hitting the road again and drag racing with the Blues Brothers." He crossed to the windows and peered through a crack in the curtains.

LuLu sat on one of the mattresses. Between the two queen-size beds was a wooden nightstand that looked as though it had been hit by one of Thor's thunderbolts. Scratched and chipped, it held a lamp, a Bible and a clock radio. She fiddled with one of the radio's knobs. "As much as I adore action adventure, I need a break from this Van Damme farce."

"Watch your language," muttered Gramps, flapping open a clean sheet.

"Van Damme the movie star," LuLu responded, raising her voice. "Not Van Damme the swear words." Gramps, a former marine, could swear a blue streak with one of his World War II buddies, but heaven forbid if she ever uttered one off-color word. If Gramps heard some of the language that went on backstage at Capri, he'd make her wear earplugs to work.

Drake stepped away from the window. "The farce is almost over. Tomorrow you'll take your test, then you can leave Vegas."

"I can't leave. I have to go into the hospital after the test, remember? If I don't get the diamond removed soon, I'll risk having appendicitis. I want to avoid that. I just hope I can also avoid having the thugs find out which hospital I slip into. I'd like to have the operation with some peace of mind." She drew a weighted breath. "I guess for me, diamonds aren't a girl's best friend."

"Right," Drake answered slowly. He seemed to contemplate this for a moment. "You have friends who can pick you up from the hospital?"

"Sure. Belle will." LuLu didn't want to elaborate on the problems she and Gramps would face then—such as where Belle would take them. How long they'd have to hide out. LuLu would have to phone Grave and makes plans to return the diamond...but he'd want money to pay off Gramps's gambling debts, too.

She rubbed her temple, wishing she could wake up tomorrow and discover all this had been a bad dream. Like Dorothy in Oz.

"Are you feeling ill?" Drake's voice pulled her from her thoughts.

"No, I'm fine. For now, anyway." She started to explain further—that the doctor had said it would be approximately forty-eight hours before she experienced any serious pain—but the look on Drake's face stopped her.

He seemed...sad. Distraught. For her? Besides Gramps, she couldn't remember the last time a man had been concerned for her well-being. She quickly looked back down and toyed mindlessly with the radio knob. "We've got things under control," she said, wishing she believed it. "You can go home now."

He should go home. And she shouldn't care. But she did. It hurt to think of never seeing Drake again. But he didn't belong here, juggling the problems of two people he'd met only hours ago. Drake Hogan was a kind stranger who had helped them out, that's all.

But he didn't *feel* like a stranger.

He felt like someone who belonged in her life.

She tugged on a curl, as though she could tug that crazy thought right out of her head.

"I guess...I should be leaving," Drake said. "You two are safe here."

Gramps, in the midst of an elaborate sheet-cornering ritual, obviously didn't hear that his new son-in-law would not be spending the night. She'd explain it all to him later.

"Thank you for your help," LuLu said to Drake, trying to sound upbeat. "And don't worry about the marriage—we couldn't be legally attached. I mean, we were the wrong couple, after all." Smiling, she hoped her appearance exuded more confidence than she felt.

"We were the wrong couple," he repeated, his voice somber.

"We were," she confirmed, not sure if she was speaking to Drake or herself.

He hitched his shoulders and looked around. "The room's on me, by the way."

"No." She stood up and fished in her pocket for the plastic Baggie. "Let me pay you..." When she extracted her hand, miniature objects tumbled to the carpet. Holding her splayed fingers in midair, she stared at the small wooden church, houses and trees that lay at her feet.

Drake held up one palm. "My treat. Besides, I don't accept doll-house remnants as payment."

LuLu bent and began picking up the tiny objects. "Never played with dolls.... This is, uh, Mayberry." From the corner of her eyes, she caught Drake nodding as though her answer was perfectly understandable.

"Mayberry," he said. "Of course."

Standing, she clutched the small objects against her stomach, not wanting to drop them again. She felt the heat in her cheeks, a telltale sign of her embarrassment that her tiny dream world had toppled for all to see. Well, for *him* to see, anyway. "Mayberry," she confirmed matter-of-factly. "The town Andy Griffith and his family lived in." She turned away, mainly to avoid Drake's questioning scrutiny, and began setting the pieces on the night table.

Drake watched her as she carefully arranged the small wooden church, houses and trees. The pieces were obviously old—even from across the room he saw the chipped green paint on the trees—yet she held each item as though it were made of crystal. For a moment, his mind flashed an image of Laura in *The Glass Menagerie,* carefully tending to her fragile dream world.

Although LuLu had her fragile side, she was also strong. Her dream world, if that's what it was, was made of sturdy wood. Maybe on closer scrutiny one might see a nick or a chip, but each piece had survived the years. Not unlike their owner, he guessed. She, too, was a survivor, thanks to her tenacity and will.

He watched her long fingers carefully arrange the small town. On either side of the church, the houses formed a semi-circle, trees filling the spaces in between. The horseshoe configuration was cozy. Safe. Was that it? This small world was safe? Guilt replaced his curiosity; he should look away. Suddenly, he felt like a voyeur stealing a peek into her innermost dreams. Indeed, her soul.

But just as he started to turn his head, she reached back into her pocket. He couldn't look away now—he wanted to know what else belonged in her safe world.

She gingerly placed three tiny objects in the center of the semicircle. He squinted. People? Because of their miniature size, each looked the same—round head, square torso, blocked legs. It couldn't be their appearance that was significant. Maybe that there were three of them?

Seemingly satisfied, she sat on the bed, leaned back on her elbows and surveyed her work. His gaze traveled from the town to her face, which had softened. Through half-closed eyelids, her brown eyes glistened with a faraway look. What did she see in that town? Who were the three people?

But he knew better than to ask. It was like asking a child to translate his or her fantasy play. Better to let them act it out, explore the moment, than to demand they explain the magic of their imagination.

He glanced at Gramps, who was busy in his own world as he straightened and wiped various objects on the far dresser. Drake wondered how often he and LuLu had slipped into their different worlds while sharing the same one.

"Before I leave," Drake said quietly, "I'll pick up some groceries from the convenience store."

LuLu turned slightly, resting her chin on her shoulder. She still had a dreamy, faraway look on her face. "Leave?" Her eyes widened as though she'd just awakened to the immediate reality. Sitting up straight, she said, "You can't pay for the room *and* groceries."

So she left her dream world when it came to practical matters. "I'll take contributions," he conceded. "But I'll do the shopping, because you two should stay in this room as much as possible."

Gramps harrumphed. "They know what you look like, too, son." He took off his apron. "Here. Wrap this around your head."

Drake did a double take at the offer. "An apron on my head? I'll look like Betty Crocker on a bender."

"This is war, son. Take it."

"If it's war, they'll think a white apron on my head is a sign of surrender. Or insanity."

"It's a disguise."

"No."

"Yes."

"Stop, you two." Huffing in exasperation, LuLu dismissed the apron with a flourish of her hand. "It's nighttime, Gramps. He'll look like a moving target with that thing on his head."

Gramps stared at the apron, scrunched his face, then nodded. "Moving target. Hadn't thought of that."

"What should I pick up?" Drake asked.

"Chocolate," Gramps declared, raising his finger in the air for emphasis.

Frowning slightly at Gramps, Drake said, "I feel as though I'm teaching my Saturday class at Peanut Butter Players."

LuLu blinked. "Peanut butter? What do you teach?"

"For money, I teach at Santa Monica Junior College. For love, I teach at Peanut Butter Players, an inner-city theater group for kids." He gave his head a shake. "Chocolate," he conceded under his breath. "Plus some real food. Be back in a few."

AFTER THE DOOR CLICKED shut behind Drake, LuLu peeked through the curtains and watched him saunter through the parking lot. Safely hidden, she could study him without fear of being caught. He was probably five-ten. Compact. Underneath that dress shirt, she imagined a solid torso, the muscles honed by...weight lifting? Tennis? Most likely the latter. From the tan, she guessed he had to indulge in an outdoor sport.

Her gaze dropped. He still wore a cummerbund, which fit snugly around his taut waist. And that butt...

Now that was a Van Damme great butt.

Forcing herself to look back up, she blew out a gust of pent-up air. Drake Hogan was lethal. Probably had a black book thicker than the Yellow Pages. A woman for every night of the week. Monday the redhead. Tuesday the blonde. Wednesday...

Just like Grave.

Old, hurtful memories stabbed through her. As she'd done a hundred thousand times over the past six years, she pushed down the emotions. Fingering the rough cotton fabric of the curtain, she focused her attention on Drake.

He strolled into a pool of light from an overhead streetlamp. Good thing he was leaving tonight, she reminded herself. The last thing she needed was a man who reeked of animal charisma, wore a tux with the ease of a high roller and drove a slick 'Vette named Sylvia.

And liked kids.

Might as well tear my heart out with my own hands and ask him to slice it in two.

"What are you thinking about, Cupcake?"

She looked away from the window. With one of the towels, Gramps was dusting around Mayberry. Few people knew that her big ol' Gramps was a hausfrau at heart. Together they had the perfect union: she brought home the bacon and he cooked it. She didn't need another man in her life.

"I'm thinking…how I want our life to be simple. Just you and me—"

A sharp yell cut off the rest of her sentence.

4

STARTLED, LuLu jumped.

Another yell pierced the air.

Was Drake in trouble?

She spun and peered through the crack in the curtains.

At the far end of the motel parking lot, under the streetlight, two teenage boys were in a standoff. The larger one, gangly and red haired, pushed the other kid, who stumbled a few feet before jumping back to his fighting stance.

Drake, who had been heading toward the alley, veered toward the kids, his hands raised in a conciliatory gesture. LuLu watched as the red-haired boy mouthed off, obviously a surly retort to whatever Drake had said. The other boy—stockier, darker, with long black hair pulled back in a ponytail—kept his fists raised, but his eyes on Drake.

When the red-haired boy lunged toward the other kid again, Drake stepped between them and blocked the punch by neatly gripping the aggressor's arm. LuLu's breath caught in her throat. She half expected to see Drake get solidly decked.

That's all we need—one comatose food scout in the Thor's Hideaway parking lot.

"Drake is breaking up a fight," LuLu said over her shoulder to Gramps, not taking her eyes off the action. "Better get ready in case we have to drag him back into the room."

Gramps harrumphed. "I told him it was a war zone out there. That's what's wrong with the world today—nobody listens to their elders."

Now the dark-haired boy sprang forward. Drake stopped him by planting his hand on the boy's forehead, as though he was catching a basketball.

Now he had one boy by the arm, the other by the head.

"Good thing there's only two. He'd have to hold off the third with a foot," LuLu reported.

Gramps was at the window now. Leaning over her, he peeked through the curtains. "What the hell does he think he's doing?"

"He's breaking up a fight. Don't cuss."

The red-haired boy tried to kick Drake, who moved in time for the intended blow to miss him. All the while, he held on to the other boy's head.

"Damn—uh, crazy fool," muttered Gramps. "Holding off two fired-up youngsters. Better luck breaking up a dogfight."

"He has a sense of honor."

"Sense of something. Foolhardiness, I'd say."

"He's no fool—he's thinking straight." *From the heart.* Drake Hogan was benevolent to others. She'd learned that firsthand. And now, she figured, that fired-up redheaded kid was learning the same, because he was calming down. She could tell from the look on his face that he was listening to Drake.

Slowly, Drake released his hold on the boy, who brusquely rubbed his arm—although LuLu doubted Drake had done any harm. The kid was probably massaging his ego more than anything else.

Next, Drake let go of the dark-haired boy, who immediately took another fighting stance.

"Round two," murmured Gramps.

"I think Drake's got it under control."

"Wanna bet?"

LuLu cast a wary glance at her grandfather. "With you? That's what got us into this mess."

"Mess?" His eyes misted over as he cautiously met her gaze. "Didn't mean to, Cupcake," he said, his voice barely audible. "I just wanted some extra money so I could replace a few tools and finish Suzie's headstone. Grave kept extending me credit at the blackjack table. And I kept losing...." He blinked rapidly, unable to finish.

She should have thought before speaking. Using the word

mess was a low blow. Besides, her grandfather wasn't a gambler. Bad with money, yes. Hard-core gambler, no. Grave had taken advantage of Gramps's obsession to finish his beloved wife's headstone. Sometimes it still baffled her how the young boy who'd offered her friendship had become a man who used and manipulated people.

"Hey, Babaloo," LuLu whispered, touching his hand. "It's not your fault—"

"Yes, it is."

She gave her head a shake. "No, Grave used you." She squeezed Gramps's hand. "What's done is done. We need to look forward—"

Laughter cut off the rest of her sentence. Laughter? LuLu jerked her gaze back outside. The boys were shaking hands. Drake stood nearby, smiling, his head cocked to one side.

She exhaled a long, slow breath. "He's okay." And charming! He'd made one of those angry kids laugh. Drake had a way with people, she thought, remembering how he'd also made her laugh when she'd been upset.

"That boy's more than okay. He's a hero." Gramps thumped LuLu on the back. "You picked a good one, Cupcake. I'm proud to call him grandson-in-law."

"He's not—"

"Got both beds made," her grandfather announced with satisfaction, shifting gears from parking-lot-reality to Gramps-reality. "Now I'll tackle the bathroom."

It was useless to remind him that Drake wasn't her husband. As he exited to the bathroom, LuLu peered through the curtains again. Both kids were strolling away from Drake. She couldn't tell which one had laughed. Didn't matter, anyway. All that mattered was that Drake, the peacemaker, had worked his charm.

For a moment he stood alone, watching the boys leave. The light raining down from the overhead lamp gave him a dramatic appearance. For a moment she envisioned him as a renegade pirate, successful after subduing the enemy.

And saving the damsel in distress.

LuLu had decided a long time ago that it was up to her,

and her alone, to make it in the world. If she didn't watch out for Number One, who would? Which meant she didn't need the help of any man. And then Drake Hogan had dropped into her life. Or maybe, she mused, she'd dropped into his. The memory of their collision made her smile. Poor guy. He never knew what hit him.

"You saved me," she murmured.

As though he had heard her words, Drake turned and stared at the motel-room window. She flinched. Had he heard? Crazy thought. Of course not.

Knowing she was hidden from his view made her bold. Inching her hand underneath the curtain, she touched the smooth glass, her fingers hot against the cool, slick pane. "That's right, you saved me," she whispered. "And saved Gramps. I didn't think knights in shining armor existed, and then you came along."

Drake, still staring at the room, raked a hand through his hair. Was he debating whether to leave this craziness? To forgo the groceries and drive back to L.A., never to see her and Gramps again? After what they'd put him through, he had every right to split.

But in her gut, she knew he wouldn't leave. Just as he'd jumped into that kids' spat and stopped further fighting, he'd jumped into her life and stopped further destruction. She hadn't even known Drake twenty-four hours, yet she believed he was a man of character. A man who wouldn't let them down.

The realization frightened even as it awed her. For the first time since Grave, she was allowing herself to trust another man. Through a film of tears, she watched Drake turn and head back to the alley. The darkness swallowed him.

"Bathroom's shoe-shine bright," Gramps announced loudly.

She swiped at her eyes before turning around.

Gramps, oblivious to her epiphany, was busy admiring his most recent cleaning job. He stood in the bathroom doorway, his six-four frame blocking her view.

"I can't believe you cleaned the bathroom with no supplies," she said, trying to keep her voice even. She still felt shaken by her thoughts.

"You're talking to an ex-marine."

She knew that explained it all in Gramps's mind.

"You know, this place could use a good overhaul." He pivoted, his arms crossed, and analyzed the peeling paint and scuffed furniture. His gray eyes narrowed under his bushy white eyebrows. "I'm surprised people would want to return to this motel."

"Well," she answered drolly, "they probably return for something other than the decor."

He flashed her a confused look. "Such as what? Hardly the maid service."

"Well…"

Gramps raised his eyebrows in understanding. "Oh."

As though on cue, they began busying themselves in silence. Gramps suddenly found it urgent to dust a chair, and LuLu picked up her bag of belongings and exited to the bathroom to change.

Fifteen minutes later, there were several sharp raps on the door. LuLu glanced at her grandfather. "Drake?" she mouthed.

Her grandfather shrugged. "X-ray vision isn't working," he whispered gruffly. "Can't see through the door."

"Very funny," she said under her breath.

"I doubt the Blues Brothers would knock," Gramps added. "Has to be Rudolpho."

"Drake," she corrected. "And since when do you know who the Blues Brothers are?" She headed to the door.

"Since Rudolpho."

"His name's not…" She stopped at the door. Leaning close, her hand on the knob, she asked, "Who's there?"

"Rudolpho."

She cast a quick glance at her grandfather, who returned an I-told-you-so look.

Shaking her head, she opened the door.

Drake, juggling two bags of groceries, nearly dropped everything upon seeing LuLu. She had changed into a pair of shorts and a T-shirt that read A Woman Needs a Man like a Fish Needs a Bicycle. He usually avoided feminists.

His gaze slid to her long, tanned legs.

Especially feminists with killer gams.

Reminding himself to tread carefully, he entered the room.

"You were great with those boys," LuLu said, closing the door behind him.

He bit his tongue so as not to say, "And you're great with those clothes." Minus the sci-fi outfit, her body's shape was obvious for the first time. Slim. His gaze skimmed her breasts. And rounded in just the right places.

He didn't want to be caught staring at her breasts, so he returned to her legs. The legs that had danced madly in hundred-something-degree heat earlier. No wonder the calves were shapely. Prancing kept the lady fit.

He imagined how it would feel to have those legs wrapped around him.

"Something wrong?" the voice above the legs asked.

Drake clutched the grocery bags with the intensity of a drowning man. "No." The single word came out garbled.

"Flow?" Gramps asked.

"No," Drake enunciated, annoyed.

He nearly tripped over Suzie before setting the bags on the dresser. Avoiding LuLu's legs, he motioned to the headstone. "As fond as I am of Suzie—" he shot a meaningful look at Gramps, who missed it because he was busy wiping a picture frame "—she's a danger in the middle of the floor."

Gramps froze midwipe. Without turning his head, he said solemnly, "Danger?"

Drake well knew that *he* was playing with danger when it came to Suzie. He'd never known a family who loved their kids—or pets—more than this family loved their headstone.

"Gramps, chill," LuLu ordered. "Drake almost tripped over her, that's all." LuLu-the-Legs crossed to Suzie. "Let's get her off the floor."

Gramps, temporarily mollified by the explanation, turned around and surveyed the room. "Good idea. She can have that bed." He motioned to the one closest to the bathroom.

Drake didn't even begin to question the logic. If Gramps wanted to put Suzie into a bed, then they were damn well going to do just that. Without a word, the three of them took their positions on the headstone, Gramps at one end, Drake at the other, LuLu in the middle. With barely a grunt—they were getting this act down pat—they carried Suzie to the bed and carefully placed her at the foot of it.

"Thanks for picking up the grub, son," Gramps said, patting the headstone and shifting his gaze to the groceries. "You got—"

"Chocolate, yes." Drake followed Gramps's gaze to the groceries, studiously avoiding LuLu. But it didn't matter where he looked in the room, in his mind he saw those long, tanned legs. She probably spent a lot of time outside. He liked that in a woman.

Here I am in a motel room named Venus, with a professional prancer named LuLu. And her grandfather, a professional war veteran and chocoholic named Babaloo.

Wait a minute, Drake thought. *I'm a wine and jazz kind of guy who courts dancers and aerobics instructors with normal home lives. But a prancer with gangsters on her tail because she's swallowed a diamond...?*

He must be losing his touch.

And he must be going. When he was back in L.A., he'd come to his senses. Call Standby Julie. Crank the stereo. Chill some chardonnay. Evolve back into the professional bachelor, his true calling in life.

But the logic didn't settle well. Something was happening to him. He didn't want to call Julie, who was always available, always waiting. Whom he kept on ice just as he did his wine. He didn't want to play his games anymore. He wanted something more substantial.

Like LuLu?

You're letting a great pair of legs get the best of you.

Giving himself a mental shake, he flipped his wrist and checked the time. "Nine o'clock." He looked up. "I'd better hop into the 'Vette and get going." For some reason, at this moment he didn't want to call his car Sylvia. "It's a long drive to L.A."

He should say something more. Something meaningful. He didn't want to just walk away from LuLu without letting her know... Know what? That besides turning his life upside down, she'd also touched him more deeply in a few hours than most women did in days? Weeks? Months? Ever.

He stuffed his hands into his pockets. *Rein yourself in, pal. This is nothing more than a dramatic situation, which appeals to your theatrical side. Plus you played the rescuer, your favorite role in life.* That's what was affecting him, not LuLu.

"Hey, thanks for the memories," he said glibly. "I'd say let's do it again, but once in a lifetime is enough." He laughed, but it came out strained.

He caught a look of sadness in LuLu's eyes. She blinked before offering a small smile. "Thank you, Drake. You were wonderful to us. We'll never forget your kindness."

Was that a look of wistfulness on her face? A show of vulnerability from the woman who outwitted thugs, married strangers and ordered around an oversize Cookie Monster? Except for the hair, LuLu reminded him of a sassy and sentimental Meg Ryan.

Her big brown eyes moistened.

A sassy, sentimental and vulnerable Meg Ryan.

His mind played tug-of-war with his heart. This was crazy—he was taking the protective-older-brother bit too far with this lady. It was one thing to help out an old man and his endangered granddaughter. Anyone with half a heart would have done the same.

That was his mind talking.

One look at LuLu's sweet, heart-shaped face and those sable eyes that glistened with emotion, and Drake was ready to camp out and play knight in shining armor for as long as he was needed.

That was his heart talking.

"We'll never forget you," LuLu added, her voice quavering.

"And I'll never forget that you flow," Gramps interjected,

effectively chilling the mood with one terse comment. "Can an ex-marine give you a word of manly advice?"

"I've never said I had to flow—"

"Flow, shmo. Say it like it is. If you gotta pi—" He glanced at his granddaughter, then swiped at his jaw as though to wipe out the word he had started to say. "I mean, if you gotta go, say go. That's what's wrong with the world today—nobody says it like it is."

I needed that dose of reality, thought Drake. *A splash of cold water on my heart will get me out the door and back to the life to which I belong.* "I'll work on it," he promised.

He dug into one of the grocery bags and retrieved a small rectangular box. "Toothpicks," he explained, dropping the box into his shirt pocket. He dug back into the bag and pulled out a soda. "And a little caffeine to jolt me awake for the ride ahead," he added, popping the top.

LuLu stepped toward him. "How many hours before you're home?"

"About six. But after Sylvia's wild ride, I might take her a little slower tonight." He took a long swig, welcoming the cool, sweet liquid.

Sweet. Like LuLu's kiss.

He swallowed hard and tried to look anywhere but into her eyes again. "You two take care of yourselves." He indicated LuLu with a dip of his head. "Call a taxi to take you to your exam tomorrow morning." He looked at Gramps. "And stay put in this room while she's gone." He wanted to add, "It's easy to pick you out of a crowd—you look like Thor himself stalking the earth." But he refrained. "Your friend Belle will take you to the hospital?"

"Sure. And pick us up, too." LuLu tugged on one of her curls. "Call when you get in? So we know you made it home safe?"

That was his line. How many times had he told some date to give him a buzz when she got in so he'd know she'd made it home safely? Too often he'd said it by rote, then taken off as soon as the lady had left. And just as often he'd returned home to find a chilly message on his answering machine, "I made it home safely. Thanks for being there so I could tell you.'' He had long ago figured it was the price he paid for being a professional bachelor.

"You'll call?'' LuLu asked again.

And how many times had he heard those same words from some woman? But LuLu didn't want him to call so she'd know she was special. She wanted him to call so she'd know he was okay. No woman had ever done that before.

"I'll call,'' he promised. And he meant it.

After one more look around the room—he wasn't sure what he was looking for; he just felt the need to make sure they were both taken care of—he left.

Minutes later, he was on Highway 15. Stars splattered the inky sky. The endless desert terrain, with all its silent secrets, lay on either side of the long road. In the spillover glow from his headlights, he spied a coyote slinking off into the gloom.

Like me. Slinking away from two people who need me.

He shoved a cassette into the tape player. He wasn't slinking away, dammit, he was driving home. He had done all he could. Hell, he didn't even know those people except that instead of painting their front door brown or white, like most folks, they painted it eggplant purple. And that instead of putting their money into a bank, they put it into Baggies. And that instead of lawn furniture, they had a headstone in their backyard.

The bluesy music of Paul Desmond filled the air. "My Funny Valentine.'' Drake smiled as an image of LuLu materialized in his mind. What kind of woman designed and wore lacy sci-fi dresses? And those shoes. Most women wore rhinestones on their ears or around their necks. Not LuLu. She had the damned things sprinkled on her toes.

She was unique, that was for sure. Unlike any other woman he'd ever met.

"Stay, funny valentine, stay....''

Drake punched the Eject button and yanked out the tape. The words of the song hit too close. To what, he didn't want to think about. He shoved in another cassette.

The soothing, moody voice of Ella Fitzgerald swirled

through the air. Lost love. Broken hearts. He ejected that tape and fumbled for another in his cassette bag.

After fingering several of the hard plastic cases, he stopped. Although it was dark and he couldn't read any of the titles, he instinctively knew his tapes by heart. He loved jazz and blues. The tape with the dent was Desmond. The scratch across the front was Ella. Nina Simone had a bubble in the top right corner of her case.

And they all sang of love and loss. Usually, this didn't faze him. Tonight he couldn't bear it.

He leaned back his head and let the rush of warm desert air flow over him. He breathed in deeply, inhaling the tangy scents of sage and dust. *Get it together, buddy. You're thirty-six. Life is filled with adventure, women, jazz, wine. Don't obsess over one woman with zero fashion sense.*

But she wasn't just one woman. She was different. Funky. Funny. Cute. Headstrong. He laughed out loud remembering how LuLu had trotted up those chapel steps all by herself. What in the hell did she think she was going to do once inside—marry whoever walked in next?

That's exactly what she'd done.

She reminded him of Meg Ryan in *French Kiss*—all spark and temper. And then, in a surprising shift, all tenderness. He remembered that dewy look in LuLu's eyes after they'd been pronounced husband and wife. How she'd kissed him on the cheek, all sweetness and femininity. He'd known her only ten minutes, yet when they'd kissed, it was as though he'd waited a lifetime for that moment.

Lifetime? Man, he'd never waxed so romantic over a pair of great legs. Good thing he was alone in this car—he probably had a goofy look that spelled *smitten* all over his face. If his pals saw him now, they'd be in a state of shock.

And he was probably allowing himself to be smitten because she hadn't fallen all over him, baked him cookies and hinted in a hundred other ways that she wanted "ever after" the way Julie and others had. No, LuLu had *bolted* after the wedding, ready to leave his life forever.

No woman had ever done that before. Not to Drake Hogan.

He laughed again.

Then stopped as a more somber thought hit him. Maybe she was spunky and independent, but her life was in danger. Yet she hadn't asked him to stay. No, she'd asked him to call her so she'd know *he* was safe. She was probably accustomed to taking care of Gramps just as Drake was accustomed to taking care of his sisters.

Could it be the two of them also wanted to take care of each other? He'd never experienced that with any woman.

He pulled over onto the shoulder of the road. With the motor idling, he drummed his fingers on the steering wheel. A car whizzed past, its red lights searing two lines of escape toward L.A.

The devil's advocate kicked in. "What are you doing, buddy? You got a great summer ahead of you. School doesn't start until fall, you got two months to sip fine wines, play tennis, date your regulars and whoever else strikes your fancy."

Strikes my fancy.

Drake shifted into first, stepped on the gas and made a U-turn back onto the highway.

KNOCK KNOCK.

LuLu, lounging on one of the beds, sat up and looked at her grandfather.

He stared back, his bushy eyebrows raised as if to say, "Beats me."

Knock knock.

LuLu charged into action. Jumping off the bed, she grabbed the wooden desk chair, which had two spokes in its back missing, and dragged it to the door. As she shoved the chair under the knob, one leg cracked and broke. The three-legged chair fell to the floor.

Knock knock.

Muttering an expletive, she bounded for the dresser and grabbed its edge. As another knock sounded, she yanked with all her might.

It moved an inch.

Knock knock knock.

She catapulted onto her bed, rolled herself in the covers and whispered hysterically, "We're going to die! We're going to die!"

Through the door they heard a familiar male voice. "It's me. Drake."

She stopped her thrashing and looked at her grandfather.

Gramps, seemingly unfazed by his granddaughter's theatrics, said calmly, "Says he's Drake this time. Wish he'd make up his mind." With a weighty sigh, Gramps got up from where he'd been sitting on the bed with Suzie, crossed to the door and opened it.

Drake stood on the doorstep, his face a mixture of puzzlement and disbelief. "What was all that commotion?"

Gramps didn't even blink. "Would you believe my granddaughter was practicing interior decorating?"

"With her, I'd believe anything," Drake said. Stepping inside, he glanced around. "Speaking of the lady, where is she?"

"Hibernating." Gramps shut the door. "You calm down Cupcake while I'm gone." He headed for the bathroom.

LuLu emerged from her hibernation under the covers. Across the room, in the dresser mirror, she saw how her hair, a chaos of wet ringlets thanks to the shower and her recent hysterics, stuck out in every direction.

"What the hell...are you...doing here?" She had trouble speaking. Breathing. She pressed her palm against her chest, hoping to quell her adrenaline rush. Drake's unexpected return had scared her. Good thing she didn't have heart trouble.

Drake shot her a quizzical look before glancing at the chair. "Didn't that have four legs earlier?"

"One broke off while I was, uh, standing on it." He was looking at her strangely. Had to be her hair. She glanced again in the mirror and patted her curls. They contracted, then sprang back into chaos.

Drake scanned the room. "What happened to the fourth leg?"

"What do you think—I swallowed it?" No way she was

going to confess that she'd attempted to dismantle the room with her bare hands. It was bad enough that her hair looked like an electrified Brillo pad. She fussed with the heap of covers bunched around her. "Why didn't you warn us you were coming back? We thought it was the Blues Brothers paying a visit."

Her hands shook as she smoothed the bedspread, but her reaction wasn't totally because she feared Grave's thugs. It was also because Drake had returned. She cursed silently, wishing he hadn't returned. She and Gramps were back to being on their own, as they were accustomed. Well, except for the fact their lives were in danger.

But having Drake back felt just as dangerous. As much as it felt good. It was as though she had been split down the middle and ripped apart. Half of her was secretly thrilled, the other half terrified.

"I should have called first," Drake answered somberly. "The last thing I wanted to do was frighten you. It's just…I couldn't leave. I had to know you were all right." He flashed her an odd look before fumbling inside his shirt pocket and extracting a toothpick.

She was shaking. He was fumbling. She wondered if they both were struggling with torn emotions.

Right before popping the toothpick into his mouth, Drake looked around the room again. "So what did you say happened to the fourth leg?"

Good. A safe conversation.

Drake quirked his head and looked at the nightstand. "Did you use it to whittle more people for Mayberry?"

Bad. An unsafe conversation. "Mayberry is off-limits," she said brusquely, regretting her bluntness even as she said the words. But Drake Hogan was treading on sacred ground by discussing Mayberry.

"Really?" When he glanced back at her a lock of hair tumbled over his brow, giving him a bad-boy look. "Even to someone who saved your life?"

LuLu felt her cheeks grow hot with embarrassment. She'd never been in this position before, having a stranger ask her questions about Mayberry. Okay, Drake wasn't totally a stranger. He was her husband. Sort of. But her private world of tiny homes and figures was a secret she kept close to her heart. Only three people had ever known what the town represented—LuLu herself, Suzie and Gramps. And that's how she wanted it. Fingering the chenille bedspread, she shrugged non-committally.

Fortunately, Gramps reemerged from the bathroom. Crossing the room, he clapped Drake soundly on the arm. "Good to have you back, son. If anyone knocks again, we'll stop LuLu from rearranging furniture."

Taking advantage of the distraction, LuLu slipped out of bed and headed to the alcove beside the closet, where she'd left her jeans.

"Yes, what happened?" Drake asked, a mischievous lilt to his voice.

At least he's off the Mayberry kick. But she wasn't sure she wanted Gramps explaining what she'd done when Drake had knocked on the door. *Be cool, Gramps,* she silently lectured. He should know how humiliated she'd feel if Drake knew how she overreacted.

"Well..." Gramps drawled, "at the end, she threw herself on her bed and gyrated."

Gyrated? He made her sound like a washing machine.

"Before that," Gramps continued, obviously on a roll, "she single-handedly pulled that dresser from the wall." He made a disbelieving sound. "Damn thing must weight several hundred pounds. But my granddaughter managed to pull it, oh, an inch before she gave up."

She yanked her jeans off the hanger. "That's enough, Baba—"

"And before *that* she ran to that there chair and dragged the sucker clear across the room to the door. At that point I was speechless, mesmerized by her rapid furniture rearrangement. Mind you, she never cleans up at home, much less moves furniture—"

"Okay, I panicked," yelled LuLu from the alcove as she shimmied into her jeans. "I heard the knock and figured it was Death paying a visit.'' Giving the zipper on her pants a yank, she stepped into the room.

Meeting her eyes, Drake suppressed a smile. "I don't think Death—or the Blues Brothers—would knock first. They'd probably just throw their weight against the door and crash into the room.''

"No doubt," she said, fighting a shiver of fear.

"Don't worry," Drake murmured. "I won't let anything happen to you.''

She wanted to say something. Meant to say something. But words escaped her. She didn't know how to respond to a man who offered her protection. A warmth flooded her, filling all the scared corners of her soul.

It took her a full moment to identify the unfamiliar sensation.

Drake Hogan made her feel something no man, even her beloved Gramps, had ever made her feel. *Safe. Protected.*

She turned away, not wanting Drake to see the tears forming in her eyes.

5

WAS LULU CRYING?

Drake dropped his gaze to the three-legged chair, grateful to have something to focus on. Knowing her, she'd be more humiliated for him to see her vulnerable than for him to see her walking stark naked through the lobby of Circus Circus.

Naked.

The leg chair became LuLu's long, tanned leg. Long, tanned, smooth, firm...

Take a detour, buddy. What did he always advise his acting students when their attention wandered? "Stay in the moment." At this moment, LuLu was upset. At this moment, she needed a friend, not an admirer.

When she expelled a weighty sigh, he glanced up.

She stood quietly, her lean form outlined against the hazy glow from the lamp on the nightstand. A line of light played along the edge of her freshly scrubbed cheek. She seemed to be deep in her thoughts. And from the downward curve of her lips, he suspected they were sad thoughts. He had no clue as to what was upsetting her, but he knew better than to ask. LuLu, with her love of action-adventure flicks, no doubt wanted to preserve her tough-girl image.

He gave his head a shake. In all his professional bachelor days, he'd never met a woman who sincerely loved Van Damme, Stallone or other hunk-of-the-month films. Most women saw those films to impress their dates. Not LuLu. She probably loved those blow-'em-up car-chase movies because she saw *herself* as the star. Well, she might envision herself as a nineties' warrior woman, but he believed that facade masked the soul of a lover—sweet, generous, passionate.

Cool it, pal. Pretend she's one of your sisters, whom you're bailing out of a problem. Crossing his arms, he studiously avoided looking anywhere below LuLu's neck. Or above. As his gaze darted around the room, he mentally repeated the magical words intended to quiet his libido.... *Little sister. Think of her as your little sister. Little sis—*

A grunt from Gramps cut off Drake's libido-quelling mantra.

"Damn—uh, darn thing is heavy."

Drake turned, half expecting to see Gramps single-handedly moving Suzie to some new resting spot. Instead he saw his huge form hunkered over the dresser, pushing—or trying to push—it back.

In two strides, Drake was at his side. With one unified shove and grunt, they placed the oversize piece of furniture against the wall.

Straightening, Gramps rubbed his bicep. "And to think our little LuLu moved Thor's dresser all by herself." Still massaging his arm, he glanced in her direction. "You got the strength of a mule team."

"Thanks," she answered drolly, not looking up.

Gramps's brow furrowed with concern. "What's wrong, Cupcake?"

"Just thinking. That's all."

Gramps studied her for a long moment. Then, with a slap of his hand on the dresser, he announced, "I think you're thinking too much. Let's check out those groceries. Something chocolate, I believe, is in order...." Smacking his lips, he turned back to the dresser and began rummaging through one of the bags.

"I didn't know how bad your addiction was," Drake said, taking Gramps's lead and keeping the tone light, "so I bought some hard-core chocolate bars and a box of mid-core chocolate cookies—flaky crust with creamy peanut-butter middles."

Gramps, one arm fully buried in the grocery bag, flashed a look at Drake. "Flaky? Creamy? You sound like a TV commercial." He fished out a red-and-white-striped box and held it up triumphantly. "LuLu? Cookie?"

She raised her head, her eyes clear—those big brown eyes that took in the world with one look. Her inner strength impressed Drake. He was accustomed to women who milked their emotional moments, pulled on a man's guilt with tears, whatever, to get their way. Not LuLu. She'd probably rather win by wrestling than by manipulating.

"Sure, I'll take one," she said forcefully.

Despite her bravura, Drake detected a quaver in her voice. Catching her eyes, he smiled, which brought a softening to her features.

"Need a can opener to get at this," Gramps griped, tearing at the wrapping on the cookie box. Drake wondered how the man cooked if he opened a box with the finesse of a bear opening a trash can. Drake glanced at the frilly, lacy apron tossed on the edge of Gramps's bed. A bear with a penchant for the finer things in life?

Drake shifted his gaze to the headstone. Then it hit him: it had to be Suzie's apron. Maybe, just as Gramps kept the headstone nearby, he kept mementos of Suzie nearby, as well. Wearing her apron when he cooked. Tucking a piece of her jewelry into a pocket.

An endless love, Drake thought. The stuff he directed in plays. But had never experienced in real life.

"Catch, Cupcake." Gramps tossed a plump cookie in her direction. She caught it in midair.

She'd make a good shortstop, Drake thought. Good looks. Sense of humor. Loved Van Damme. If Drake overlooked her sewing skills, she'd be pretty damn near the perfect date.

"Heads up, Rudolpho," Gramps called out. A cookie sailed toward Drake. He snatched at it, fumbled and missed. The chocolate confection smashed against the far wall with a soft thud.

"Babaloo," LuLu chided softly, "give the guy a little notice, would you?" She winked conspiratorially at Drake while biting into her own cookie. As she chewed, she closed her eyes and made what he swore was a small purring sound. He had the momentary urge to be reborn a bakery item in his next life.

When he caught another flying cookie, he felt like part of the Headstone Clan again.

For the next few minutes, the three of them munched in silence. It felt comfortable. And despite their situation, happy. Drake thought back to when he'd last felt this way. Years ago, he decided. Not since his days at home with his family. He caught another cookie, and after riding a macho wave of accomplishment when LuLu smiled at his success, he decided to stop grinning at her like a twelve-year-old boy who'd just made the team. Dropping his gaze, he reread her T-shirt. A Woman Needs a Man like a Fish Needs a Bicycle.

"What are you looking at?" she asked.

He swallowed the rest of his cookie before answering, "That T-shirt. Where'd you get it? At a fish rally?"

She half smiled. "You're kidding, right?"

"Bicycle rally?" He knew he was being silly, but he liked making her smile. Liked how a dimple came to life in her cheek.

"Ever hear of Gloria Steinem?" she asked.

"Was she in *Under Siege?*"

LuLu narrowed her eyes. "That was Steven Segal."

"I meant the female costar."

"You're impossible."

"I've been called worse."

"Incorrigible."

"Getting closer."

After she brushed some cookie crumbs off her chin, her eyes locked with his. "Bad boy."

"Bingo."

"I'm not a gambler, you know," Gramps said gruffly, interrupting their conversation.

In unison, LuLu and Drake looked at him. "Join the club," Drake said.

"Babaloo, what does that have to do with the price of tomatoes?" LuLu asked.

"Thought I'd say something in my defense." Gramps scratched at his chin and avoided their eyes.

"Oh." LuLu smiled knowingly. "We weren't talking about

gambling. Drake said 'Bingo' because I guessed one of his nicknames.''

Gramps frowned, his forehead compressing into stacked folds. "He's called Bingo, too?"

Drake narrowed his eyes as though trying to focus on this awkward conversation. "Actually, Bad Boy."

"Bad boy?" Gramps repeated, his baritone voice rising. He gave his massive head a shake. "I refuse to call you that. Rudolpho, okay. Bad Boy, no way in—" He shot a look at LuLu. "No way in the world. Makes you sound as though you have to be housebroken." His bushy eyebrows raised as a thought hit him. "But considering that flow problem, maybe there's a reason you've been nicknamed Bad Boy."

"I *don't* have a flow problem—"

"Could someone toss me a cookie?" LuLu interjected sweetly. "And change the subject while we're at it?"

As Drake again started to refute Gramps's statement, and as Gramps started to burrow into the cookie box, LuLu experienced a swell of nausea. When the room suddenly tilted, she groaned and clutched her middle.

Drake dashed across the room and caught her as she lost her balance. In one smooth motion, he gathered her into his arms and carried her to the bed. Laying her down, he commanded, "Call 911."

Gramps lurched toward the beige phone at the end of the dresser, then stopped. "Son," he said, pivoting to face Drake. "The hospital's close. We could get her there faster than it would take some damn ambulance to get here."

"I'm okay," LuLu said defensively. "Just a twinge in my tummy."

"More like a diamond in your gut." Sliding his hands underneath her, Drake started to lift her.

"No!" LuLu said fiercely. Shoving him back with one hand, she scooted to the other side of the bed. "If we go, I'll miss my test in the morning."

"If we don't go," Drake responded, "you might miss the rest of your life. Appendicitis is serious."

LuLu swiped at a wayward curl that had tumbled over one

eye. "The doctor said I'd run a slight fever, maybe feel some nausea for a few days before anything...critical happened."

"This is more than a slight fever." Drake reached for her again.

She scrambled to her feet. "It passed. It's over. I'm back to the slight-fever stage."

"You're more hardheaded than a..." Drake muttered something under his breath. Then he wagged his forefinger at her. "Quit acting like a petulant child and let me help you to the car." But his fury abated when he saw the frightened look in her big brown eyes. "Please, LuLu," he added gently. "Let me help you."

"It's just that..." She ran her tongue along her lips. "If I go into the hospital tonight, I'll miss my exam in the morning. There's not another exam for almost six months...." She squeezed her eyes shut, then slowly reopened them. "In six months, I'll have lost the chance to work as a reflexologist at a new casino and spa that opens in two weeks. They've offered me *twice* what I make now. Plus I'll no longer have to work at Capri. For Grave." She stared for a long moment at Drake, her eyes filling with tears. "I *need* this job. It means freedom. Money. And one day..." She winced and shut her eyes again.

Taking advantage of her not seeing him, Drake crossed to the other side of the bed and scooped her up before Gramps could say, "Flow, shmo."

"Gramps, open the door," Drake said, holding LuLu firmly in his arms.

"Damn you, Drake!" LuLu thumped his chest with her fist.

"If you were stronger, I might have felt that," he answered calmly as he carried her toward the open door.

She fluttered her legs. "I'll kick. I'll scream."

"Go ahead."

The warm night air surrounded them as he transported her outside. When they were almost to the Corvette, Drake looked over his shoulder at Gramps, who toddled behind, looking more terrified than LuLu. Drake sensed what was going on with the older man. He'd already lost his Suzie. If he were to lose LuLu also, his life would be meaningless.

"Gramps, help me get her into the car."

As Gramps helped Drake ease LuLu over the passenger door and into the front seat, Drake noticed the older man's hands were shaking.

"It's going to be okay," Drake said calmly.

"It's not going to be okay when I tell the hospital you kidnapped me!" LuLu tried to open the passenger door, but Gramps kept it firmly closed by leaning against it.

"Cupcake," he said authoritatively, "let your husband take care of you."

"Husband?" She expelled a gust of air in disgust. "He wishes."

Drake bounded to the driver's side and opened his door. "What I *wish* is that you'd behave until I get you to the hospital." He jumped in and slammed the door shut. "You make me glad I teach theater and don't drive an ambulance for a living," he muttered under his breath.

She crooked an eyebrow at her grandfather. "Did you hear him? He teaches theater. Probably does to actresses what Grave does to showgirls."

Drake started the engine. "I'll pretend you're delirious with fever and didn't mean that." He looked at Gramps. "Where's the hospital?"

Gramps pointed toward the street that ran in front of Thor's Hideaway. "Take a right at the thunderbolt. Go two, three miles until you reach the first major intersection—"

"This is ridiculous." LuLu huffed loudly. "It's only a little nausea—"

"Take a left at the intersection. It's a mile, tops. On your right."

"Got it." Drake shifted into reverse.

"Call me," Gramps ordered.

"You two are acting as though I don't exist," LuLu complained, crossing her arms tightly under her breasts. "A little dizziness is no reason to overreact."

"Will do," Drake replied to Gramps. Backing out of the parking space, he said between clenched teeth to LuLu, "And

I don't want to keep reminding you that it's more than a little dizziness. It's a diamond wedged in your appendix."

LuLu rolled her eyes heavenward. "I liked it a lot better when the three of us were throwing cookies."

Drake waved to Gramps, a two-fingered, it'll-be-okay salute.

"I love you, baby," Gramps called out as they pulled away.

LuLu turned in her seat. Her grandfather stood in the parking lot, looking tall, formidable, yet somehow broken. Like a fallen giant. "I love you, too," she whispered before the Corvette bounced over an ill-placed speed bump and squealed out of the lot.

She sank down into her seat. All she really had in the world was Gramps. As much as she wanted a better job, a better life, without Gramps it would mean nothing. Lowering her head, she fought the urge to cry.

Drake touched her hand. "You okay?" he yelled.

Rather than compete with the blast of wind, LuLu simply nodded. In the passing light of overhead streetlamps, she caught the look of concern in Drake's eyes. She felt a twinge of guilt that she had accused him of boffing actresses.

Maybe Drake was right—maybe she spoke rashly because she was delirious with fever. She touched her forehead. It felt normal. Well, as normal as a head could feel with hot air blasting at it. She didn't want to think what her hair would look like by the time they made their grand entrance into Emergency. They wouldn't know what to treat first—her dizziness or her deranged hairdo.

A red light was ahead. Good. After they stopped, she'd explain to Drake that she really and truly felt okay. A little nausea never killed anyone. Besides, she *had* to take her exam in the morning. If anything was life or death for her, that was.

They eased to a stop. She sat up. Plastering a smile on her face, she said, "Drake, I don't—"

Her head jerked back as Drake stomped on the gas and the car roared through the intersection. Palm trees, homes, streetlamps were a blur of color and light. She was vaguely aware of the scent of jasmine.

Why go to the hospital? He might as well drive straight to the morgue. Enough was enough.

"Drake!"

No response.

"Drake!"

Shifting gears, he glanced at her. The wind blew his dark hair over his brow, giving him a devilish look.

As though he needed it.

She was attempting a yell when something glittered in her peripheral vision. She looked ahead. Another red light.

He stepped harder on the gas.

With a scream, she covered her head and doubled over. Sylvia peeled rubber through the intersection. A car horn blasted. A jumble of swear words, interlaced with "California driver," faded into the night air as the lawbreaking Sylvia careened down the road.

LuLu straightened, avoiding Drake's questioning gaze. She'd explain her preference for adhering to traffic laws after they got to the hospital.

A few minutes later, the hospital complex emerged on their right. With relief, LuLu inhaled a deep breath. This crazy ride was almost over. When they pulled up in front of the Emergency entrance, she planned to leap out of the car and kiss the ground. Emergency personnel would probably send her to the psychiatric ward first, but she didn't care. With any luck, they wouldn't let Drake follow her.

She allowed herself a small grin. They were at the hospital now. Even in a psychiatric ward, life would be sane again.

Drake turned sharply into a large parking lot. Sylvia spun and shuddered, her tires screeching.

Life sane? Maybe not.

LuLu gripped the grab bar. "We're there! No need to play Mario Andretti!"

Of course Drake didn't hear. Wouldn't heed her panic attacks anyway because this was a guy on a macho mission. She glowered at him, conjuring up images of all the tortures she'd inflict after she was out of this mess. Top of her list: get hold of his little black book and mix up the phone numbers.

That would serve him right—calling blondie and getting brunettie by mistake. That would put a crimp in his style.

The Corvette veered left. LuLu toppled over, the stick shift poking into her side. Wincing, she pushed herself back into a sitting position, ready to yell no matter what forces threatened to gobble her words. But then something caught her eye.

On the far side of the hospital parking lot she saw the word *EMERGENCY* in big red letters over what looked to be double glass doors. So that's why Drake had made that gut-lurching turn.

God, she missed her trusty bicycle.

They barely missed an Audi that crossed in front of them. Oblivious of the near collision, Drake continued to race forward at the speed of fright.

Try to think positive, LuLu told herself, as she wondered if that rattling sound was her bones. He might actually stop the car and not drive straight into the hospital.

Her heart jumped. But this time not from the erratic driving. Ahead, in front of the glass doors to the Emergency entrance, stood a black lump in a Hawaiian shirt.

The short thug.

LuLu pointed wildly with one hand while thumping Drake's arm with the other.

"Hang on!" he yelled, dipping his head her way. "We're almost there!"

She continued to point as Drake squealed the car to a mind-numbing stop at the curb right in front of the short thug. For a moment the world stood still. The thug, half a doughnut in his hand, blinked. LuLu, for some reason, couldn't lower her hand, which seemed to be frozen in permanent point mode. She had no idea what Drake was doing behind her—undoubtedly joining her in staring down the thug.

Stereo stare down. Without music.

The thug, a smudge of powdered sugar on his chin, gave them a spider-to-the-fly leer.

"God, I need a toothpick," Drake said, breaking the silence. He shoved the car into gear, slammed on the gas, and Sylvia was off and running.

LuLu retrieved her pointer finger and hunkered down in the seat. Peeking cautiously over her shoulder, she saw the thug throw down his doughnut and gesture at them with wild, pumping motions. Too bad he didn't just keel over right there. Those Emergency personnel would have him strapped down on a gurney before you could say, "Hawaiian shirts don't go with suits."

No such luck. As though jolted with an electric cattle prod, he suddenly stopped his flailing and dashed into the parking lot. She prayed that Madonna, the gold Chevy, was at least thirty parking spaces away.

LuLu turned back to Drake and yelled, "He's following us!"

He glanced at the rearview mirror before shooting her a confused look. "Bus?"

LuLu leaned closer, started to speak, but changed her mind. She'd probably repeat the message only to have Drake ask, "Cuss?"

They turned right out of the hospital parking lot, tires burning, and zipped along a four-lane street. To the left, bordering the far two lanes, was a high wall of shrubbery that LuLu recognized as the leafy boundary of a golf course. This was a different route than they'd taken here—hopefully Drake had a good sense of how to get back to the motel. If not, she'd help him with points and jabs.

Fortunately, the motel wasn't that far away. LuLu breathed in a deep breath of warm summer air. Safety and Gramps were close. If she got out of this mess intact, she'd make a pact with Gramps to live a boring, predictable life for the rest of their days.

She shifted her gaze slightly to the right. Overhead streetlights sparkled along a shiny gold hood.

Madonna.

And Short Thug.

She swallowed back a sour taste in her mouth. Should she nudge Drake? Where would he go? With her luck, he'd swerve left, drive through the wall of bushes and onto the golf course.

No matter what, this little car chase was going to get ugly, fast.

They were rapidly approaching a large intersection, where streams of cars crisscrossed. No way could Drake pull one of his infamous through-the-red-light numbers. No, he'd have to stop at the light. And so would Shorty.

She squeezed her eyes shut, fighting images of gunshots and blood. She had to do something. *Now.*

The Corvette eased to a stop.

LuLu opened the passenger door. Behind her, she heard Drake yell, ''What the—?'' She also heard a grunt. Probably Shorty, post doughnut digestion, articulating some primal killing urge.

Time felt hopelessly slow. Picking up one leg after another, LuLu hoped she was sprinting and not walking. She veered around the end of the Chevy and jogged to the far side of the street.

Behind her it was ominously quiet. Drake and Shorty having another stare down? If the thug had stayed put, that is. Maybe he was already out of the car, running after her.

If so, she hoped that doughnut was part lead.

Gulping air, LuLu quickened her pace. Bounding in front of a blue Honda, she caught the driver's bewildered look. A few steps later she leaped onto the sidewalk. *Run run run!* Another sound kept time with her pounding feet: thump thump thump. It was either her galloping heartbeat or the slap of Shorty's feet behind her.

Don't look. It'll slow you down.

Pumping her legs harder, she zigzagged across a circular driveway to a residential home. Gravel crunched under her feet. A dog barked. Ahead there was a white fence—one of those adobe numbers with lacy bricks. With a small prayer that there were no Dobermans on the other side, she leaped up and scrambled over the wall.

DRAKE, HEARING THE passenger door open, had glanced over in time to see LuLu bound out of the car. He'd started to call out when his gaze collided with two familiar beady eyes.

Shorty.

Sitting in Madonna.

LuLu. Looking back, Drake caught her jogging behind the Chevy, across the lane and into oblivion.

At the sound of a slam, Drake looked back. Shorty had exited Madonna. Gun drawn, he was jogging after LuLu.

"Hey, jerkface," Drake yelled.

The short thug paused and looked back.

Drake knew he could get shot, but didn't care. All that mattered was to buy time for LuLu.

"I got the diamond!" The traffic light flashed green. Drake stomped on the gas. It would take the thug a few moments to get back into his car. Precious moments that Drake would use to divert attention away from LuLu. Hopefully, Shorty wouldn't use the next few minutes to figure out it made no sense that the diamond would have miraculously moved from LuLu's appendix to Drake's car. Remember, Drake told himself as he shifted, thugs were thugs because they had noodles for brains. Hardly the type of guys to go to medical school.

In his rearview mirror, Drake spied the thug getting back into the gold Chevy. Damn, traffic was slow. Still, it would take a few moments for the thug to get started and back onto the racetrack.

Drake jerked the wheel to the left and nearly spun as Sylvia skidded toward what looked to be an alley. He cut right in front of a white Audi and a Winnebago. Horns blasted. Brakes screeched.

He was getting used to such noises.

As Sylvia careened down the alley, Drake tightened his grip on the wheel. Usually he had the homing sense of a pigeon. But after a maddening rush to the hospital, followed by yet another life-defying car chase, he wouldn't know due north if a compass was embedded in his brain. *So what if I'm lost,* he thought, *I'll probably be dead any minute.*

My last day on Earth spent saving Orphan Annie and Daddy Warbucks. He shifted, swerved right onto a side street and sped past a fast-food store. And no last meal. All he'd consumed in the last twenty-four hours was two cookies. Three, if he hadn't missed the first one.

He jerked the wheel left and veered down another side street. Sylvia bumped and shuddered as the left wheel hit a curb.

Lost. Hungry. And facing a car repair bill that would kill him if Shorty didn't. "I'm never getting married again," he yelled into the wind.

FORTY MINUTES LATER, Drake knocked on the door to Venus.

After a pause, a gruff response came from the other side. "Who's there?"

"Rudolpho."

The door swung open. There stood Gramps, his face lined with concern. He looked past Drake. "Where's my grand-daughter?"

Drake stepped inside. He'd driven like a madman for the first ten minutes, then parked in some stranger's driveway, neatly hidden by a row of assorted cacti and bushes, for several more before inching back onto the street and finding his way to Thor's Hideaway. He was certain he hadn't been followed.

He sank onto the edge of LuLu's bed, exhaustion and adrenaline warring within him. "She's..." He rubbed his chin, not knowing how to explain. He decided that trying for tact was a waste of time. Honesty was best. "She's somewhere in Vegas."

Gramps stood stock-still. "What?" His voice rolled through the room like thunder.

A storm was quickly approaching.

Drake looked up at Gramps. "She jumped out of the car and ran away before I could stop her," he explained calmly, although he didn't feel that way inside. "She wanted to escape from the short thug, who was in a car next to us. I diverted him away from her, fortunately."

"Fortunately?"

The older man hadn't asked a question. The single-word

response was laced with sarcasm and fury. Drake didn't blame him. This was a hell of a mess.

He raked a hand through his hair. Could he have stopped her? In his mind's eye, he saw LuLu leap from the car and dash off into the night. She was impetuous. But smart. She'd find her way back. In his gut, Drake believed that, as certainly as he and Gramps were in this room. LuLu would make it back.

"She'll be okay."

"Okay?" Gramps repeated in the same disbelieving tone. "My sweet baby's out there alone, sick, on foot, and you have the *balls* to say she's okay?" He stomped several steps across the room, stopped, then smashed the air with his fists. "Okay? How the hell do you know she's okay, you…" He battled the air again, his face red with the exertion.

The storm had hit. He had to keep a handle on this crisis. "We have to believe she's okay," he said gently. "It's all we have to hold on to right now."

"Bull. You shouldn't have returned here without her." His chest heaving, Gramps dropped his arms and glared at Drake. "That's what's wrong with the world today. Nobody takes responsibility. I'm going to find her."

Drake leaped from the bed and stood in front of Gramps, blocking his path to the door.

"Get out of my way," Gramps warned. He took a fighting stance.

"Gramps—"

"You got *that* name right." He raised his balled fists a notch.

"If you go out there," Drake said carefully, "there'll be two of you on the loose, doubling the chances of the thugs doing harm. We need to wait here. LuLu will be back soon. I promise you."

"You *promised* to take care of her. But instead, you gambled with her life."

It hit Drake that earlier, in his vows, he *had* promised to take care of her. And even though he was a diehard non-gambler, Gramps was right. He'd gambled with LuLu's life. Slowly, he opened his hands as though he had nothing to conceal. "I'd never do anything to hurt LuLu."

"You didn't do much to *help* her tonight, either."

"I carried her to the car. I rushed her to the hospital."

Gramps's gray eyes misted over. "That's what...what..."

When, after several moments, he didn't finish his thought, Drake prompted, "What?"

Giving his head a shake, Gramps cleared his throat. "That's what I did...for Suzie." Lowering his fists, he looked over at the headstone. "I carried her to the car," he said hoarsely. "I rushed her to the hospital. But...it was too late...."

The two men stood in silence. Gramps, his broad shoulders slightly rounded, continued to stare at the headstone. Drake remained in front of him, his hand poised in midair. He wanted to comfort, but didn't want to intrude.

He couldn't stand that the older man felt so alone at this moment. That's how Drake had felt when his dad died. It had been tough being ten years old and suddenly thrust into the role of man of the house.

He laid his hand on Gramps's shoulder. "I'm sorry," he said. "I'm so sorry."

Gramps nodded brusquely, keeping his face turned. Then, slowly, he raised one huge hand and laid it on Drake's. "Thanks, son." He paused. "I'm sorry, too. Sorry I overreacted. I know you did your best tonight. You love LuLu just as I do."

Love?

A soft knock sounded.

Gramps raised his head and eyeballed the door. "Did I hear...?" He started for the door, but Drake stopped him. "We still have to be careful," he warned in a low tone. "Who is it?" he asked, raising his voice.

"Harriet."

Drake headed for the door, but this time Gramps stopped him by firmly clamping him by the neck. "She said Harriet."

"The counterpart to Rudolpho," Drake explained. "Trust

me, the thugs couldn't sound that sweet if they sucked on honey for a month.''

Gramps and Drake almost stumbled over each trying to get to the door first. At the last moment, Drake stepped back and let Gramps have the honors. With his face cracked open in the largest grin Drake had ever seen, he pulled on the door so hard that Drake thought for sure it'd come off its hinges.

LuLu, standing quietly outside, smiled. A broken twig stuck out of her hair. One shoulder of her T-shirt was ripped. A dark smudge streaked her cheek.

''Any cookies left?'' she asked weakly.

6

SLUMPED AGAINST the doorjamb, LuLu cast a weary look at Gramps, then Drake. "Don't ever take me to the hospital again. I'd rather swim the Amazon with one hand tied behind my back."

She trudged into the room and fell facedown onto her bed. The soft chenille spread, smelling slightly of must and perfume, was comforting after scaling walls, running on gravel and inhaling exhaust.

Behind her, the door clicked shut. Then a large, warm hand rested lightly on her back. "You okay, Cupcake?"

Gramps. He was trying to sound calm, but she heard the worry in his voice. Turning her face slightly, she looked at him. "Babaloo…" A piece of chenille fuzz tickled her nose. "I'm—I'm—" She scrunched her face in anticipation of a sneeze.

"Drake, hospital!"

"Right," Drake said.

Footsteps. The bed sank under someone's weight. Hands slipped underneath her. Drake, the macho body scooper, was ready to whisk her into his arms. Hospital déjà vu flooded her mind. Red lights. Short thug. More gravel. She didn't need to escape Grave's bad guys; she needed to escape these two do-gooders.

Clutching her grandfather's hand, she fought the sneeze while trying to say, "No." But she sounded more like Belle's cat when it gobbled its peanut-butter-coated vitamins.

"It's that damned diamond in your gut," Gramps explained as though it was news to her. "We have to get you to the hospit—"

"Gramps, open the door," Drake said, lifting her.

Hadn't they heard her Amazon preference? LuLu squeezed hard on her grandfather's hand. "No!" The gobbling episode had passed. She could form words again.

With a grunt she squirmed out of Drake's hold, plopped onto the bed and rolled over onto her side to face him. Blowing a curl out of her eye, she said tightly, "It's not the diamond. I made a face because I had to snee—snee—"

She sneezed, blinked, then fell back onto the bed. Staring up at the peeling ceiling, she said calmly, "If you two want to do something useful, please check my knee. I fell on some damn gravel...."

There was a pause—probably as the do-gooders realized she wasn't having an appendicitis attack. Gramps finally mumbled something about her knee.

"Looks a little roughed up," he said, tenderly touching her leg. "But not bad enough to cuss," he admonished under his breath.

"I'll get a washcloth," Drake said, crossing to the bathroom.

"I think this is a special cussing occasion," LuLu said, watching Drake's exit. "When you're wounded in battle, it's okay to cuss. A little." She figured her grandfather, who lived every day as though it were D day, would appreciate her logic.

"Oh, baby." Gramps's face hovered over hers. His gray eyes, which usually had a hint of the rascal in them, were clouded with worry. Deep grooves lined his forehead.

She patted his arm. "Gramps, just kidding about the battle. It was only a minor skirmish."

"It could have been worse," he said, his voice breaking. With a trembling hand, he cupped her face. "We might have...lost you."

Lost. How she and Gramps had clung to each other after losing Suzie. LuLu had done everything in her power to keep him focused on living—took him on walks, to movies, and one night out of sheer desperation, to a Wayne Newton concert. She'd kept Gramps busy for months; otherwise, she knew she'd lose him, too.

And then, a year later, when Grave broke her heart, Gramps had consoled her. How many nights had they sat up until the wee hours, drinking lemonade, while Gramps counseled her about men and love? Not that he was an expert, he'd often repeat. He'd had only one true love, his Suzie, but forty years of marriage had given him some insights.

During those talks, they'd also discussed LuLu's dreams. That was when she'd decided reflexology was her next career, for two reasons. First, she liked a profession that helped people. Second, after she built a clientele, she could work out of her home. With a decent income and the ability to be at home most of the time, she figured a court would be more favorable to her adopting a child.

Remembering those late-night conversations, she reached up and smoothed back Gramps's mane of white hair. In her peripheral vision, Drake's face materialized. His blue eyes reflected the same concern as her grandfather's.

"Let me look at that scrape," he said gently.

Gramps hesitated, then stepped back to give Drake room. LuLu wondered if it was difficult for Gramps to watch another man take care of her—even if that man was her "husband."

As Drake sat on the edge of the bed, her gaze traveled over his tux attire. After a crisis wedding, multiple car chases and a stint as ambulance-driver-from-hell, Drake Hogan looked as cool and collected as James Bond after saving several nations and getting the girl.

Dabbing at her knee with the damp washcloth, Drake said, "So you played kneesies with some asphalt?"

"With a brick wall, if you must know."

He cocked one eyebrow, but kept his attention focused on her knee. "That's original."

"That's me."

A smile cracked his serious countenance. "Yes, that's you all right," he said in a low tone.

A low, sexy tone. The kind James Bond used when tending some bikini-clad heroine in some exotic locale. Not some heroine in a ripped T-shirt and a tacky motel room named Venus. Not that LuLu was jealous of the James Bond girls. No-o-o.

But someday, when she looked back on her life, it'd be nice to see a few moments when she had oozed sensuality. To see herself reflected in a man's eyes as an enticing woman with allure, not as an overaged tomboy with a scraped knee.

LuLu sighed heavily.

Drake lifted the cloth. "Did that hurt?"

"Are you hurting, baby?" Crowding Drake, Gramps leaned forward, his face etched with worry.

The enticing-woman fantasy popped. Suddenly, she felt like Dorothy at the end of *The Wizard of Oz,* lying in bed with the human counterparts of the Tin Man and the Cowardly Lion hovering over her. Drake, the Tin Man, who desperately needed to know he had a heart. And Gramps, the Cowardly Lion, who had more courage than he realized.

"I'm okay, you two," she said with a smile.

Drake's gaze inched slowly over her, from head to toe. "Any other scratches or hurts we need to doctor?"

A spark fired to life inside her. The mild throb in her knee took a back seat to the rush of heat that flooded her insides. She wished her body would behave itself and respond to its physical aches rather than its libidinous ones.

"No need to play doctor." Play? It'd be nice if her mouth behaved, too. "I mean *be* doctor. No need to *be* doctor." She realized she was clutching the chenille bedspread with all the finesse of a cat clinging to a tree limb.

Drake's eyes held hers. Within those blue depths, she saw a tenderness that confounded, yet warmed her. Drake—James Bond with a souped-up 'Vette—didn't seem the type to exhibit such compassion.

"She was always getting scraped and cut as a kid," Gramps said gruffly. "We weren't sure if she'd grow up to be a boy or a girl."

"So I compromised and grew up a tomboy," she quipped, glad the conversation had steered in another direction.

"No wonder you like those action-adventure flicks," Drake said. "You're *still* a tomboy at heart." He pulled a small leaf out of her hair and held it up for LuLu's inspection. "What other secrets are tucked in those soft curls?" he asked huskily, tossing the leaf into a trash can next to the bed.

Her breath caught as Drake toyed with a loose tendril of hair that lay against her cheek. He brushed it out of her face, but let his fingers linger. "Can't find any more secrets," he murmured, "from your wild night on the town."

She wanted to say something saucy, a retort far better than any of Bond's bikini girls could conceive, but her thoughts melted into one incoherent lump when he gently cupped her cheek in his warm palm.

"I'm sorry you had such a tough night," he said quietly, tracing a path along her cheek.

Her skin burned underneath his fingertips. She tried to concentrate on something, anything, other than his warmth and tenderness. But her world had shrunk to a small cocoon of sensation where all that mattered was Drake Hogan's touch.

With great effort—more emotional than physical—she pulled away from his caresses.

"Any cookies left?" she asked shakily.

Gramps jumped to attention. "My baby needs cookies."

As the older man headed toward the grocery bags, Drake tossed the washcloth onto the nightstand. "She also needs something nutritious, Gramps," he said, his James Bond tone reverting to the man-in-charge voice. "Dig out some of those oranges, too."

During the next thirty minutes, between munching on cookies and oranges, LuLu recounted her wall-scaling and traffic-dodging feats to make it back to Thor's Hideaway. Her story was punctuated with, "That's what wrong with the world today—too many thugs," from Gramps and, "From what action flick did you learn that trick?" from Drake.

"And then I knocked on the door, praying you two were inside Venus waiting and not outside in Vegas looking for me." She sat up in bed and brushed the last few remaining cookie crumbs from her hands.

Gramps, one hand over his heart, the other resting on the headstone, said solemnly, "We were worried sick about you."

"So was I," added Drake, who still sat on the edge of her bed.

LuLu smiled to herself. Drake, who had earlier acted as though she and Gramps had some kind of cemetery fetish, now accepted Suzie as the fourth member of this party.

"Well, I'm pooped." LuLu stood and looked at the clock on the nightstand. "Almost midnight. Test is at ten tomorrow morning. Time to hit the sack."

After a moment's hesitation, Drake eased off the bed and stood. "And I should hit the road." He rubbed his jaw as though debating whether or not to say something. Finally, he said, "You're calling a taxi to take you to your exam, right?"

"Just as we discussed," LuLu answered.

"And your friend Betty—"

"Belle."

"Will pick you up after the exam and take you to the hospital?"

LuLu nodded. "She's a fast driver. I figure if she and I spot any vagrant thugs, we can skip that hospital and shoot to another. Worse comes to worse, we can hit all six Vegas hospitals in a matter of hours."

"Thought you didn't like to drive fast."

"Unlike *some* people, Belle knows red means stop. It's a plus."

Drake shot her a sharp look before continuing. "And she'll pick you up from the hospital as well?"

"No," LuLu said with exasperation. "I was thinking I'd hitchhike."

He sent her another quelling look. "Have you called Belle to set up all this hospital hopping?"

She glanced at the clock. "It's kind of late to call her now. I'll call her first thing tomorrow morning."

Crossing his arms, Drake continued to gaze at LuLu. "And what if she's not in?"

"I'll leave a message."

"And if she doesn't call back right away?"

LuLu crossed her arms, too. "Since when did you become my mother?"

"Since you bowled me over." His heart lurched. *Bowled me over.* What had his buddy Russell said to him earlier today? *Mark my words. Some lovely damsel will bowl you over.* Drake saw LuLu as though for the first time. Had he ever noticed the glints of gold in those crazy auburn curls? Or the coral tinge of her lips? He still remembered the tentative brush of her lips against his after they'd been pronounced man and wife. It was supposed to be a kiss to fool the minister, but its sweet intensity had been unnervingly real.

He returned his gaze to those big brown eyes, remembering how they'd blinked in surprise after the two of them had toppled to that hot, hard sidewalk.

He'd been bowled over, all right.

"What are you thinking?" she asked, arching one eyebrow.

"That I hadn't expected to meet a damsel today."

"No cussing," Gramps interjected.

LuLu ignored him. Instead, she glanced down at her torn T-shirt and scraped knee, then back to Drake's eyes. "I thought damsels wore gossamer and tiaras."

"Well, this is the nineties," he said drolly, uncrossing his arms. "A damsel needs a tiara like a woman needs a—a…"

One corner of those coral lips quirked in a self-conscious grin. "Like a woman needs a man to drive her to an exam."

"Look," he said, shifting his tone from whimsical to no-nonsense. "I think I should stay over and drive you to the exam tomorrow."

"I'm not helpless."

In her short response, he heard volumes. LuLu didn't want to be viewed as needing him. He glanced at the slogan on her T-shirt. Or needing any man.

"I'll grab an extra blanket and pillow and camp out on the floor," he said matter-of-factly, turning toward the closet.

"My index finger isn't broken. I'm capable of calling a taxi."

"True." He opened the closet door. "But you are also capable of being grown up enough to accept help when it's genuinely offered, right?" He glanced over his shoulder and caught her pursing her lips, as though fighting what she wanted to say next. "Tonight I belong here. End of discussion."

She shot him a look of severe disapproval.

"LuLu, baby," Gramps said, "your husband is being a real lollapalooza. Accept his help—even if he does say damn too much."

"Fine," she said tightly, never taking her gaze from Drake's.

"My pleasure," he answered, knowing her relinquishing control was probably more painful than she cared to admit.

"Did you use this in-charge approach when you stopped those boys from fighting?" she asked defensively.

Funny. The "end of discussion" line worked with his kid sisters. And with a few argumentative dates. But obviously not with LuLu Van Damme, the hardest head in the West. He grabbed several light wool blankets. "You were spying on me?"

"We both were," Gramps admitted. "You're a diplomat, son. Proved it with those hooligans. Proved it with me, too, when I tried to deck you."

When Drake turned around, blankets in hand, he caught LuLu staring at her grandfather in disbelief. "Deck?" She looked back at Drake. "While I was out there dodging the forces of evil, you two were in here *duking it out?*"

Drake juggled the blankets from one arm to the other. "We were, uh—"

"I got steamed," Gramps explained in an earnest voice, his arm draped comfortably around Suzie. "But your husband eighty-sixed the fight." He gave Drake a sharp salute. "You can take command anytime, son."

"Eighty-sixed?" Drake repeated. He still wasn't sure when this conversation had taken a sharp right.

"Means the kitchen ran out of something," LuLu said, still giving both of them a disbelieving once-over. "Or in this case, you made sure the fight ran out of ammunition." She gave her head a shake. "I can't believe you two almost resorted to such a macho maneuver as a fistfight."

Drake crossed to the far side of the dresser. "We were worried about your well-being." He dropped the blankets onto the floor. "Besides…" He cocked her a challenging look. "I can't believe you, a fan of action-adventure flicks, dare to scoff at macho maneuvers."

Her mouth opened as though she was going to say something, then closed. "I'm going to take another shower," she said tersely before marching to the bathroom.

Drake allowed himself a small smile. LuLu's toughness didn't alienate him. If anything, it intrigued him. He had the distinct impression she needed it to shelter her fragility. And sometimes to conceal her love of macho maneuvers.

Thirty minutes later, they were all nestled into their respective beds: Gramps in one with Suzie at the foot, LuLu in the other, Drake against the far wall across from LuLu's bed.

He'd stripped down to his underwear. The pleated shirt, along with his pants, lay draped over the three-legged chair. The rented tux was starting to get the grunge look, but tomorrow was the last day he'd have to wear the damn thing. He'd noticed that LuLu had shed the feminist-slogan T-shirt for an oversize, plain white T. Probably Gramps's. Drake liked how it outlined her pert and rounded breasts.

"I'm turning off the light now," LuLu warned, patting the covers around her.

Click.

Darkness.

"Before we go to sleep…" Gramps said, his voice booming through the room.

Drake, lying on his makeshift bed, wondered if the resulting ringing in his ears was permanent.

"Gramps," LuLu said sweetly. "You don't have to talk louder because it's dark."

Click.

Light flooded the room.

Gramps sat up and cleared his throat. His mass of white hair sprang from his head, giving him the look of a senior-citizen troll doll. "Before we go to sleep," Gramps repeated, dropping his voice a decibel, "I just wanted to say that this is your…" He cracked one of his knuckles.

"Your what?" LuLu asked.

Gramps folded his huge hands demurely in his lap. "This is your wedding night," he said quickly. "And the last thing you two need is an old man hanging around." He paused. "An old man and Suzie," he corrected, glancing at the headstone. He looked back at his granddaughter. "After we're out of this mess, I'll get my own place. You and your husband take the house. After all, it's yours, Cupcake."

Now LuLu sat up. "It's *ours*," she said in a determined voice. "*Our* home for the rest of our lives."

Gramps puffed out his cheeks before speaking. "I meant, now that you're married and ready to raise a family, you don't need an old man getting in the way."

"I need you in the way more than ever! And besides—" she motioned toward Drake "—that man and I aren't—"

Gramps raised his hand, halting the rest of her sentence. "Yes, yes, I know you two haven't, uh, officially been together as man and wife yet—"

"People," Drake interrupted. He sat up, joining the impromptu family powwow. "Can we go to sleep? LuLu has an exam in the morning and then she has to go into the hospital. Gramps, you're not in the way. LuLu, we're not raising a family. End of story. Turn out the light, please."

He lay back down and shut his eyes. These two were more chatty than the kids at one of his sisters' slumber parties. He sighed, dimly aware of the silence in the room. He'd probably offended someone, again, but didn't care. It'd been a hell of a long day. He needed some *z*'s.

Click.

Darkness.

Within minutes, Gramps was snoring. The droning climbed several pitches before leveling out into one long staccato snort. Drake stared at the ceiling, trying to count sheep, but instead wondering what was louder—a lawnmower or Gramps.

"Drake, you asleep?" LuLu asked softly.

She had no idea how seductive her voice sounded in the dark. He recalled other times a woman had spoken those same words to him, but the question had always involved an ulterior motive. "Not anymore."

She moved around in the bed, the rustling of covers more distracting than the snoring. Drake's mind filled with images of long, tanned legs intertwined with sheets. He turned onto his side, wishing the rug was thicker. The hard floor offered little comfort for his predicament.

Gramps did a three-tiered snore that ended in a prolonged wheeze.

"I didn't go over my notes for the exam," LuLu whispered urgently.

He shifted to look at her, all the while mentally cursing the motel management for investing in cheap carpeting.

A thin stream of light seeped through the crack in the curtains. The silver line—part moonlight, part streetlight—streaked the side of her bed and disappeared into the folds of the covers heaped over LuLu's form.

How he'd like to disappear into those folds as well.

"Do you have your books with you?" he asked. *Stay focused on her exam. Forget the folds.*

"Forgot to pack them."

"That's understandable. We were trying to escape two gangsters."

LuLu giggled.

He smiled, recalling the dimple in her cheek when she laughed. It was nice to hear her being lighthearted again.

"Sorry I scared you two tonight," she said. "But at the time, jumping out of the car made sense."

"Did you really think it through first?"

Drake listened to the distant hiss of traffic—interrupted by bursts of Gramps's snores—as LuLu delayed her response.

"Not enough time."

He had the feeling that if she had all the time in the world, she'd still act on impulse. He'd never met a woman who relied more on adrenaline than common sense. "Let me give you a bit of brotherly advice. Next time you're faced with a decision, take a breath before you rush into something."

"You're giving me brotherly advice?"

He again eyed the thin silver line that coiled into her covers. Had he ever envied moonlight before? "You'll do well on your test tomorrow," he said reassuringly, opting to sidestep the other thread of conversation.

"I could practice on my feet if they weren't so sore from scaling walls and trotting across gravel."

"Practice on your feet?"

"Reflexology."

"Right." Reflexology, criminology, long-legged-babe-under-the-covers-ology. They were all the same to him.

"I could practice on *your* feet," LuLu suggested.

Drake bit his tongue so as to not say something he'd regret. He had a million comebacks for her line. *You can practice on me anytime. You can practice on my feet and more. Practice, baby, practice.*

When he didn't say anything, LuLu said, "I meant practice *reflexology.*"

"That's what I thought you meant," he answered quickly. Too quickly. Had she heard his thoughts? "Let's practice," he said, hoping he sounded all-business. He gave himself a mental pat on the back for not twisting his words into a sexual innuendo.

He heard her slide out of bed. Gramps's snoring had evened out into a low-range hum. The lawnmower had evolved into a distant vacuum cleaner.

LuLu opened the drapes slightly. Moonlight poured down on her. "Over here," she whispered, sitting on the floor between her bed and the window.

He was dressed in boxer shorts only. Hardly decent attire for a first date. If Gramps woke up and found them seminaked, playing reflexology on the floor, what would he do?

Nothing. After all, he thought Drake and LuLu were married.

Drake pulled back his blanket and edged over to where LuLu sat, wondering if any other man had spent his wedding night playing footsie.

He moved in closer and sat cross-legged in front of her. The light played tricks with his eyes. LuLu's skin, which he knew to be lightly tanned, glowed like alabaster in the pearly light. And within her heart-shaped face, those big brown eyes took on a depth, a mystery, just as night kept secrets from day.

It felt otherworldly viewing her nocturnal beauty. As though he'd stepped into a dimension where LuLu-the-Tomboy had been transformed into LuLu-the-Temptress.

"You're beautiful."

"You're incorrigible," she whispered.

"No, Bad Boy."

"Well, Bad Boy, give me your bad foot."

He extended his leg. Time to snap out of it. Realign his sensibilities, which he probably could do if her touch wasn't like warm liquid against his skin. Or if she didn't stroke his feet with such soft, expert fingers.

He was doomed.

"Any problems?" she asked.

"Yes. I'm trying to be good but my foot's being bad."

"I meant," LuLu whispered emphatically, "any health problems you'd like me to work on?"

Watch it, buddy. Don't blow it with one of your come-ons.

"Uh, not really."

She kneaded his foot. Ripples of sensation started at his feet and skittered up his spine. This was better than the time he'd dated that toe sucker. What was her name? Shauna? Sheila? *Sh*-something.

A wave of hot pleasure rolled over him. "Shazam."

"Your shoulder, right?"

He leaned back on his elbows and tried to pinpoint the core of good feeling he had just experienced. Damn. She was right. His shoulder didn't feel as tense.

"Left shoulder. How'd you do that?" He, who was always in control when it came to women, had become putty in her hands.

"Each foot—and hand, too—has five longitudinal zones that correspond to different parts of the body," she whispered matter-of-factly, oblivious to his putty status. "The shoulder extends from beneath the crease between the fourth toe and the little toe—" she positioned her fingers "—and extends down to just below the ball of the foot." She moved her fingers in a firm, rolling motion. "Breathe in," she instructed.

If she had told him to tap-dance on the ceiling, he would have. He breathed in. Another wave of warmth radiated around his left shoulder. A groan escaped his lips.

"You weren't supposed to breathe out yet."

"I wasn't breathing. I was groaning."

"Try to concentrate on what we're doing," she said peevishly.

You don't know how hard I'm trying. He raised up a bit and looked at her. Although the oversize T-shirt hung loosely over her torso, he again deciphered the curve of her breasts. Small, round. The kind that filled a man's palm just right. Curling underneath the bottom of the T-shirt were those long legs that ought to have a permit to be seen in public.

He imagined gently pulling her down to the floor, his body firmly on top of hers, molding to hers, and inching his fingers underneath that T-shirt....

"What are you thinking about?" she asked.

"Molding and inching."

"What?" She stopped massaging his foot.

"I mean, I have a pain in my—" *libido* "—gallbladder."

"Really?"

He forced a small laugh. "Made it up—" An unexpected, multitiered snore cut off the rest of Drake's thought. Good. It gave him time to figure out what he was doing, seminaked on the floor with a beautiful woman, talking about gallbladders. When the snore subsided, Drake whispered, "Thought making something up would help you with your exam."

He could hardly admit the truth—that sitting in his boxers with LuLu massaging his foot was more arousing than any other romantic situation he'd ever been in. Hands down over the time he and Amy-the-Cheerleader played first-and-ten, which until tonight had been number one in his ten hottest memories.

LuLu giggled lightly. "Making up things to help me? You're sweet."

Sweet?

He was a dog for lying to her. She deserved better than that. He thought of all the times he'd fudged the truth to women. Told them another girlfriend was just a friend. Or that he was playing poker with the boys when he was actually taking a date to the symphony. *That* little lie had come back to bite him big-time when the woman he'd lied to saw him at the symphony with his date's head resting on his shoulder. He could hardly write off Ms. Head-to-Shoulder as a cousin or a pal. To this day, he couldn't listen to Saint-Saëns without feeling a pang of guilt.

"Breathe in, slowly," LuLu instructed, pressing the middle of his sole.

"I'm sorry I lied."

LuLu looked up. "About your gallbladder?"

"The symphony."

"What does that have to do with your gallbladder?"

"I didn't know Colette would see Julie's head on my shoulder."

LuLu stopped momentarily and looked at him. "Just tell me there was a body attached. I hate to think you have a thing for disembodied girlfriends." Under her breath, LuLu murmured, "I've never had someone experience a flashback while I'm practicing reflexology." She pressed again on his foot. "Breathe in. If I knew where your conscience was, I'd work on that, too."

He breathed in, surprised about his remorse. He'd never regretted his actions before. Was guilt tied to one's gallbladder? He'd better not name any more organs. He'd probably undergo excruciating grief if his spleen was reflexologized.

His gaze wandered over LuLu's lithe form as she tended to his foot. Her hair had tumbled forward, obscuring those features he'd come to adore: those saucerlike eyes, those ripe lips. He imagined a life of slowly breathing in...

"Now, breath out."

And out.

And taking out the garbage.

And making out...

And making love...

All night long. Her sinuous body cradled in his arms, those killer legs intertwined with his, the look of pleasure on that sweet face as she looked up at him. Hot, passionate lovemaking every day, every night for the rest of their lives....

Rest of their lives?

"What are you pressing?" he said edgily. This wasn't reflexology. This was witchcraft.

Gramps snorted, like an exclamation point following Drake's question.

"Shh," LuLu warned, looking over at her grandfather, who shifted and wheezed before settling back into his distant-vacuum-cleaner drone. "Did I hurt you?" she asked, looking back at Drake.

"Is there a marriage bump on the bottom of my foot?" There was probably a wedlock-zone that she was pressing.

"Are you okay?"

No. "Yes." *Damn.* He squeezed his eyes shut. He was lying again.

"Marriage bump?" she repeated under her breath, tracing a line down the bottom of his foot. "Maybe I accidentally slipped off the gallbladder into another area...."

He shuddered as her fingers inched down the arch of his foot to the heel. Gallbladder, liver, spleen—he'd heard that the way to a man's heart was through his stomach, but through his other internal organs...?

He opened his eyes. "I think you have the foot thing down," he said, withdrawing his. "You'll do well on your exam." He made a mental note to never again submit to reflexology. One more session and he'd end up with four screaming kids in a battered Winnebago careening toward some vacation mall in Minnesota.

LuLu's hands remained open for another moment before she dropped them to her lap. "I touched something you didn't like," she said matter-of-factly. She leaned forward and peered into his face.

She was close. Too close. He could smell the scent of soap on her skin. Sense the texture of her silky hair. He rolled his tongue in his mouth, imagining what she'd taste like. Sweet, fresh...

"Sometimes reflexology is more effective than a person anticipates," she whispered.

Her voice had dropped to a sexy range that, in Drake's past, had meant satin lingerie and lovemaking. Not oversize T-shirts and reflexology.

"I probably should have discussed it more with you up front," LuLu added.

He didn't want to lie again. Not to LuLu. "We should probably discuss a lot of things."

"Such as?"

He was in this deep, so might as well go for broke. "How we...feel about each other." Damn, that was the kind of line women said to *him*. He exhaled a pent-up breath. *Say it like it is, buddy. If you're going for truth, don't stop now.* "You make me think of things I've never thought about with a woman."

"Such as?"

"Taking out the garbage." Okay, that was a partial truth. But who said he was supposed to reveal the entire story in act 1?

"I shouldn't have pressed your gallbladder."

"I think it's attached to my heart."

"What?" She gave her head a shake. "No, the heart is in a different longitude—on your left foot, straight down from the fourth toe."

He took her hand. "I'm not thinking about longitudes. I'm thinking about...what it would be like to wake up with you every day for the rest of my life." He ran his fingers along the inside of her palm. "Unfortunately, I'm not the marrying kind."

He should have signaled that abrupt turn in the conversation, but it took even him by surprise. Telling the truth was becoming a bad habit.

"Neither am I." LuLu's soft tone had a distinct edge. "Except on a whim with a stranger when my life's at stake."

She started to withdraw her hand, but Drake tightened his

hold. "I'm sorry." God, he'd never meant it more. LuLu was the last person on earth he wanted to hurt. "If there was ever a woman—"

"Let's not go there." LuLu gave her head a firm shake. "Been there. I can take the truth. Prefer it, actually."

"The truth is, my past works against me. I became the man of the house when I was ten. My mother worked two jobs trying to raise five kids. It was tough. Never enough money. I swore I'd never get married and raise a family…because what if something happened to me? I can't bear the thought of leaving behind a similar legacy."

For a long moment, they simply sat, their fingers loosely intertwined. "I can't bear repeating my past, either," LuLu said. "My mother and father were always on the road. When I was growing up, my best friend was the TV. After my parents died in a car accident, Gramps and Suzie moved in to take care of me. For the first time, I understood the meaning of family. Not in the traditional sense, but in the Mayberry sense…" She started, obviously having said more than she meant to.

"Mayberry?"

After a beat, she said, "Yes, Mayberry. My town."

Her voice sounded as though it came from a long way off. Maybe because her mind had drifted to her small dream world. "Tell me about Mayberry," he gently coaxed. "Why does it have three figures?"

She dropped her head, as though thinking through whether she wanted to divulge her secrets. Finally, raising her head a notch and meeting Drake's gaze, she said softly, "In Mayberry, there was Opie, Aunt Bee and the Andy Griffith character. I loved that show. Because my parents were always on the road, almost all I did was watch television. When Gramps and Suzie moved in, they didn't want me living my life through sitcoms and soap operas, so they took the TV away."

"That must have hurt."

"It helped that Grandma Suzie bought a small wooden town to replace my favorite TV town."

"Mayberry," said Drake thoughtfully. "And you, Gramps

and Suzie—just like Andy Griffith, Aunt Bee and Opie—were the three figures...."

"Yes."

"But Suzie's..."

LuLu nodded her head, understanding the implied question. "I see the three figures a little differently now. They're me, Gramps and a baby."

"A baby?"

"I want to adopt. You know, like Rosie O'Donnell. Lots of single women do that these days."

"I like kids, too, but why not wait for the right guy to come along and make it a real family? It's a tough enough world without raising a kid single-handedly." He could instantly tell that he'd stepped in it with that comment. Even in the stream of moonlight, he saw LuLu stiffen. She lifted her chin a notch in defiance.

"Sorry," he said, holding on to her fingers, which threatened to pull away. "Growing up with a single mom, I have too many memories of the tough times. I can't tell you how many years after my father died that I'd blow out my birthday candles with the single wish, 'I want my Dad back.'" He leaned forward and whispered huskily, "But I shouldn't judge you wanting your own child. My apologies."

Her profile softened. He even thought he caught a small smile of acceptance. "I'm surprised you don't want kids," she said softly. "You were good with those boys in the parking lot. They weren't easy to corral, but you did it."

"Comes from volunteering with an inner-city theater project for kids—I usually stop a few fights before they settle down and enjoy playacting. Eventually, I'd like to be a child psychologist. Help kids who grew up like me...you know, a little on the rough side, needing some guidance."

LuLu made an approving sound. "We're not so unalike. We both want to create a good environment for children."

"We both want another thing, too," he said slowly. "A life without hardships."

"And loneliness."

They sat in silence for a long time, holding hands. Outside, the distant hiss of traffic remained constant.

But between him and LuLu, something had irrevocably changed. Without stating it in words, they had agreed that their infatuation had reached an end because neither of them could take a chance on love.

7

LuLu BLINKED OPEN her eyes and stared up at the peeling ceiling. Another wave of nausea washed over her. She swallowed, hard. This queasiness had to pass. *Had* to. She probably shouldn't have jumped out of the car last night. Trotting through traffic and scaling walls weren't the healthiest of activities for a gem-toting woman. Especially when the gem was stuck in her appendix.

Drake was right. She acted before thinking.

She shifted her gaze to the clock. Eight o'clock. She had two hours before her reflexology exam. Time to get ready and fake that she felt fine. Because if she didn't fake it, Drake and Gramps would have her stuffed into the Corvette and driven at breakneck speed to the hospital before she could say "gallbladder."

Gallbladder. She closed her lids. What had Drake said about his last night? "I think it's attached to my heart."

She opened her eyes. Strange line from a James Bond type. That or he had never studied biology. She breathed in and out several times, wishing away her queasiness.

After pulling back the covers, she eased onto the floor. The pumpkin-tinted rug felt coarse under her bare feet. The thick curtains, still opened from her impromptu reflexology practice last night, offered a long rectangular view of the parking lot. On the cracked asphalt was sleek Sylvia, looking like a sophisticated lady sitting primly in the middle of a bus stop.

Glancing away, LuLu caught sight of Drake on his makeshift bed across the room—a mass of bronzed skin and black hair with blankets wadded around muscular thighs. She quickly turned back to the window, feeling more invigorated than if she'd had a caffeine transfusion. Was he *naked*?

After several moments of replaying the heady mix of tanned skin and body hair in her mind's eye, she grew aware that her nausea had disappeared.

Maybe looking at naked men was a good thing.

Maybe it was a miracle.

She'd be written up in the *National Enquirer*. "I was sick, and then I looked upon a naked man and I was healed." Women would no longer go to Lourdes to take the waters; they'd go to Chippendale's to take the waiters.

She stared out the window at Sylvia, but looking at a buffed Corvette just didn't do the trick. Okay, she wanted to check out Drake again. Just one peek. It wasn't as though she was *flirting* with him. After all, they'd agreed last night they could never be an item. Besides, who would ever know?

Behind her, a low, methodical wheeze told her Gramps was deep in dreamland.

And Drake, who was asleep, would never know because she'd never confess. *Never.* She'd be on her deathbed and if someone asked if she'd ever looked upon a naked man while he was sleeping, she'd say, "Just once. But it was under *strict* doctor's orders."

On her deathbed, *lying*. Was that any way to end one's life?

She shifted her gaze and caught a flash of muscled thigh.

Yes.

Besides, if it had gotten rid of her nausea, this time it'd probably clear up the scrape on her knee.

Holding her breath, she slowly turned her head to get a better look.

Drake lay on his back, one arm lifelessly at his side, the other limp across his torso. A muscular, Thorlike male specimen with nothing on...but a pair of boxer shorts.

Okay, partially naked. It wasn't as though she was ogling a butt-naked guy. No, she was merely checking out a semiattired man. Couldn't be worse than looking at one of those celebrity boxer ads. Any twelve-year-old girl could open a magazine and see some star in boxers. In the grand scheme of things, sneaking a peek was a rather innocent act.

So innocent, it wouldn't be a big deal if she got a better look.

She leaned her head forward while keeping her body facing the windows. In case he woke up, all she had to do was snap her head back and pretend she'd been staring through the crack in the curtains. If he asked why, she'd say she'd been watching over his beloved Sylvia. That would earn *big* brownie points with Mr. Stud Muffin.

She craned forward for a better look. Ah, this was better. *Much better.*

Ooo. This man could be a stand-in for Van Damme any day. He had the body of an athlete. Toned. Fit. Forgetting her Sylvia-brownie-points excuse, LuLu swiveled toward the object of her fascination—it was too difficult facing north while her body strained west. A woman was not meant to be a compass.

Very carefully, so as not to make a noise, she scooted down to the end of the bed for a closer look. After all, this was probably the last time she'd ever see an almost-naked man. Not counting Van Damme and Stallone, of course.

Biting her lip—in case she accidentally moaned—she scrutinized Drake's body.

Black, curly hair spread over his chest and tapered to a V right above the band of his boxers. As he breathed in and out, those solid pecs swelled slightly. She stroked the chenille bedspread, imagining how it would feel to press her hand against that naked chest.

She stopped stroking and frowned. How many other women had pressed palms against that body? He'd mentioned Julie. And Colette. And, of course, there had been the infamous Sylvia. So far, six palms and counting. He probably had more palm imprints than Grauman's Chinese Theater.

Probably seen more lingerie than a Victoria's Secret salesperson.

And probably gazed into more women's eyes than an optometrist. Women who stared back with undisguised lust. And

wore perfect makeup. And dyed their hair shades of champagne. Women with external beauty—like Sylvia—but with
little internal substance.

LuLu yanked a thread out of the chenille spread.

Men were like that. Give them the box and forget the prod-
uct. No way *she'd* be a number. No way *she'd* look at him
with desire. No-o-o, her looking him over was simply out of
idle curiosity. It had been awhile and she was simply—simply...

Heat fluttered within her. Her heart thumped.

She was simply...aroused.

She tried to tuck the faded pink thread back into the spread.
Okay, maybe she was looking at him with a *little* lust. After
all, it had been a few years since she'd been with a man. She
mentally checked off how many. Six? One probably reverted
to being a virgin after five. So be it. She couldn't have weath-
ered another relationship after the hurtful affair with Grave.

But just because she wasn't buying, didn't mean she
couldn't window-shop.

Pleased with her spur-of-the-moment philosophy, she sat on
the edge of the bed and stared boldly at Drake's face, wishing
she could have seen how he'd looked last night when he'd
said he'd like to wake up with her every day for the rest of
their lives. But the room had been hazy with shadows and
moonlight—impossible to read the message in his blue eyes.

His eyelids fluttered a little as he slept. No man had a right
to have such thick black lashes. She liked how they cast spiky
shadows on his high cheekbones.

Her gaze traveled down to his chiseled nose and stopped
on a small white scar that creased the bridge. A scar? Mr.
James Bond had a flaw? It was reassuring to know he was
human.

As she smiled at the thought, her gaze caressed his mouth,
recalling the way he crooked one side of his lips in a sexy
grin. And what was it with the toothpicks? She'd never met
anyone who always needed a stash of them nearby.

Her gaze recklessly slid over his chin and back down the
mass of black curly chest hair to the waistband of his boxers.

Silk?

She licked her dry lips.

The man wore baby blue silk boxers. Where before heat had fluttered, it now sparked within her.

She should stop here, at the boundary of blue silk. To look further would be trespassing upon his manhood.

She glanced at Gramps, who was still snoozing.

Back at Drake, who was probably dreaming of Grauman's Chinese Theater.

And back to the top of those baby blue silk boxers.

Holding her breath, she inched her gaze over the waistband to the bulge swathed in blue silk. He seemed nicely... proportioned.

She dipped her head to one side. From this angle, he looked bigger. She dipped her head the other way. From this angle, bigger still. Strange. Was it her nausea returning? Maybe it was warping her eyesight.

She straightened and blinked. *Okay, inventory's over. Get ready for the exam.* After one last, lingering look at the anatomically correct boxers, her gaze traveled swiftly back up, over the molded pecs to those startlingly blue eyes.

She gasped.

Those startlingly blue, *open* eyes.

"Enjoying the view?" Drake asked sleepily, a suggestion in his voice that thrilled her even while it embarrassed her.

She meant to say something in her defense, but when she opened her mouth, only a strange squeaky sound came out.

Drake smiled. Not a cozy good-morning smile, but an I-caught-you-in-the-act-you-devil-you smile.

Maybe it hadn't been her imagination that the bulge bulged.

She cleared her throat, but knew better than to try and speak again. If she resorted to a series of high-pitched squeaks in front of this guy, she'd never forgive herself. Best tactic, as Gramps would say, was a hasty retreat.

With a defiant toss of her head—but given her nervousness, it probably looked more like a twitch—she stood.

"Tweetie?" Drake said in an incredulous tone. He raised up on one elbow and stared at her tummy.

Tweetie? She looked down. Nothing was on her tummy except Gramps's wrinkled T-shirt, which was wedged in a most unladylike fashion into the front of her undies.

Her Tweetie Bird and Sylvester undies.

For a small, excruciating eternity, she kept her head bent, staring at the little cartoon characters that cavorted on her waist-high, 100-percent-cotton underwear. The kind of underwear babes with no sex life wore.

She pawed at the T-shirt. If she hadn't still been suffering from severe baby-blue-silk heat flutters, she might have been able to get the damn T-shirt unwedged from Tweetie and Sylvester.

Frantically, she glanced up. Drake coolly checked her out, a sexy grin teasing his lips. She'd have walked—no, stomped—away if she thought her legs would cooperate. But she had the crazy premonition that if she took a step, she'd fall flat on her face. And then he'd see Tweetie from both the front and the back.

"Nice undies," Drake said in a husky undertone.

She squeezed her eyes shut, humiliated to be exposed in front of a man who wore silky blue boxers while she sported Looney Tunes cotton.

She sure knew how to impress a guy.

"I would have thought," Drake continued, "that you'd pick ones with Van Damme kicking rather than Tweetie Bird hopping."

She gave Gramps's T-shirt one last tug, wishing the damned thing would grow an extra three feet and reach her knees. "We're even," she said between her teeth. "Now please turn your head so I can exit to the bathroom."

"I'd rather watch."

"Try flipping to the cartoon station."

"There's no TV. Besides, Tweetie never looked so good."

Heat flamed her cheeks. "Bad Boy." She meant to say it with disgust, but the words came out breathy. Needy.

"Sometimes. But right now I'm a gentleman, so I'll turn my head." He winked saucily at her before looking away.

She picked up one foot. Good. Her balance was intact. She

marched to the bathroom, not caring if she woke Gramps. Damn Drake, anyway. She'd be glad when he was back in L.A. with his bevy of Bond girls and their assortment of lacy panties.

By nine, she and Drake were dressed and ready to go. She took no small satisfaction that Drake was forced to wear a two-day-old rented tux, whereas she was wearing a clean blouse.

Gramps was sitting up in bed, adjusting to the new day. He was wearing his favorite red pajamas, which probably was the first thing he'd packed despite their flight from gangsters and guns.

"Slept like a baby last night," he said in his megaphone voice. He squinted at Drake. "How'd you sleep?"

Drake, who was returning the folded blankets to the closet, said, "A plank provides more cushioning than that carpet."

"Plus you were snoring, Gramps," LuLu added.

Gramps raised his bushy eyebrows in surprise. "Me? Snore? Suzie never complained."

"It's those earplugs she wore," said LuLu, "which is why she never told you to lower your voice, either."

"Lower?" Gramps lips formed an O of understanding. "Lower," he repeated, dropping his voice several notches.

Drake, closing the closet door, tried not to think of other things that were lower. Such as LuLu's cute undies. He imagined his fingers playing chase with Tweetie and Sylvester...things he shouldn't be imagining. After all, they'd reached an unspoken understanding last night that they could never be more than...than what?

Friends?

Gangster escapees?

Husband and wife for a day?

He turned to look at the woman who was all of the above, and more.

Cross-legged on her bed, she wore jeans and a yellow blouse decorated with red, white and purple flowers. With her feminist T-shirt and her love of action flicks, it surprised him that she owned *anything* feminine and flowery. Just when he thought he had her pegged, she surprised him.

"Drake's driving me—" she flashed him a warning look "—hopefully following the speed limit—" she looked back at Gramps "—to my exam. Should be back by one."

"One?" Gramps glanced at the clock and pouted. "What am I supposed to do while you two are gone?"

Drake thought Gramps looked like a little boy who was fretting about being left home alone. He wondered if this was a scene he and LuLu played out often.

"Now, Babaloo," LuLu said sweetly, "there's plenty of food. Plus Suzie's here. You can have your morning coffee together." She glanced at Drake. "Gramps starts each day with a cup of coffee and a chat with Suzie."

Drake wanted to say, "No need to explain," but instead just nodded. "Sorry there's no TV," he said apologetically to Gramps, recalling LuLu's earlier line about flipping to the cartoon station. He caught himself smiling. Not too many women threw out comebacks as fast as LuLu.

Gramps shrugged. "Don't miss a TV at home. Don't miss one here."

"As I told you, I watched so much as a kid that Gramps and Suzie banned it when they moved in," LuLu explained, standing. "At first I whined and carried on, but eventually I got used to it."

"Like learning not to add salt to your food," Gramps confirmed. "Life is distracting enough without an electronic box blasting all day long. That's what's wrong with the world today—too much TV."

"Listen to the radio while we're gone," LuLu said. "We'll be back before you know it."

Gramps squinted one eye while pointing a warning finger at Drake. "This time return with my granddaughter."

If she doesn't leap out of the car again. "I'll do my best."

"Best isn't good enough." Gramps's voice carried a warning.

Drake fished in his shirt pocket and popped a toothpick into his mouth. "I'll bring her back," he said around the toothpick, all the while shooting a don't-make-me-a-liar look at LuLu.

Those big brown eyes, wide with innocence, met Drake's threatening stare. She smiled sweetly. "Shall we go?"

Minutes later, they were pulling out of the parking lot. After last night's dramatic emergency-room send-off, Drake had asked Gramps to stay in the room. It was risky enough for any of them to be outside in broad daylight. Las Vegas might be a big city, but Drake didn't want to take more chances than necessary that they might be spotted by a wandering thug.

He typically kept a scarf in his glove compartment so a date could wrap it around her hair and not get windblown, but one of them—after a tiff—had charged off with it still on her head, so bye-bye scarf.

Drake eased the car to a stop at the entrance to Thor's Hideaway. "Sorry I don't have anything for your hair."

LuLu glanced at him, her eyebrows pressed together. "You carry hair spray? Rollers?"

"I meant a *scarf.*"

"Oh." She looked back at the road. "Did one of your women make off with it?"

One of my women. As though I own a truckload of 'em. He rolled the toothpick from one side of his mouth to the other.

"It makes sense," LuLu said, sharing a ripple of her stream of consciousness. "You're the type of man who'd think of a woman's needs. Like keeping a scarf in your car."

Was she skilled at backhanded compliments, or was it a side effect of speaking her mind? "Which way is your reflex thing?" he asked, ignoring her comment.

"Do you know where Cranberry World West is?"

"They hold these exams at fruit stands?"

LuLu narrowed her eyes. "So you didn't like my 'women' comment—no need to make fun of my future profession." Not waiting for his response, she pointed at the two-lane blacktop road in front of them. "Take a left to Eastern. When we hit Warm Springs Road, take another left."

Draft shifted and stepped on the gas. "You still haven't explained how fruit and reflexology go hand in hand."

"You still haven't explained which woman made off with your scarf."

"It wasn't *my* scarf. It was a generic you're-in-a-convertible-use-this-scarf scarf."

LuLu held up her fingers and twiddled them in the wind. "If anyone has the right to be *testy* today, it's me."

Even though he caught her impish grin out of the corner of his eye, he ignored her play on words. "You seem to think I'm Casanova."

"James Bond, actually." She dropped her hand. "Cranberry World West, by the way, isn't a fruit stand," she said, returning to their previous conversation. "The exam isn't there, but nearby."

It was a lazy, peaceful morning. A roadrunner scurried across the road ahead. Drake chewed on her James Bond comment, and the end of the toothpick, as they cruised slowly down the street. When he realized she had grown unusually quiet, he looked over and caught her staring at the toothpick.

He down shifted to a stop sign. "What's wrong?"

"Are you addicted to toothpicks?"

"Addic—?" He cocked one eyebrow. "Only the ones that have been dipped in exotic drugs. You know, the kind James Bond likes."

"He doesn't do drugs. He does martinis."

She probably knew the habits of every action-adventure star since the advent of the talkies. "I recently quit smoking."

"Hard to believe you smoked in the first place."

She turned her tanned face toward him. He liked how the sun gleamed on her chestnut curls. And how open her face was—like a sunflower. No guile. No gimmicks. With LuLu, what you saw was what you got. Unlike other women, with whom you had to peel away layers before you understood the core person.

"Why is it so difficult to believe I smoked?"

She shrugged. "Lots of women don't like kissing a smoker." She gestured with her hand as though it was self-explanatory.

Lots of women? "No one ever complained."

"Of course not. What are they going to say? Kissing you is like licking an ashtray?"

He tossed down the toothpick with a bit more force than he intended to. With LuLu, what you heard was what you got, too. "Have you ever filtered any of your thoughts? Or do you always blurt out whatever's on your mind?"

She raised one eyebrow. "You *are* testy today." She lifted her foot and fiddled with the shoestring. Sunlight glinted off the rhinestones that dotted her sneakers.

He flicked his wrist. Nine-fifteen. No cars around. He could spare a few moments to set Ms. Rhinestone Shoes straight. "First of all, I don't have a James Bond complex—"

"I never said compl—"

"And secondly, I've never had a woman complain about kissing me, whether I was smoking or not."

With a look of amusement, LuLu pressed her finger against her lips.

"What are you doing?" He heard the edge to his words, but didn't care. LuLu was a handful. Either she was jumping out of cars or running off at the mouth.

"I'm filtering my thoughts."

Despite his irritation, he smiled. She had a knack for angering him one moment and humoring him the next. "Good," he said softly. "You should practice more often."

Those brown eyes snapped at him. But as she removed her finger to say something, he stepped on the gas. The churning motor and the swirling desert air made conversation impossible.

One point for James Bond.

Twenty minutes later, he pulled up in front of a square, pinkish adobe building. Painted on its front wall was the imprint of a foot; circling it were the words *What's Afoot Reflexology Center.*

"This is it," LuLu confirmed.

"No kidding."

He parked on the street behind a van, which he guessed had been originally painted blue. It was difficult to see the color through all the multicolored hand- and footprints that decorated its exterior. In the back window hung an American flag. The license plate read FOOT0D8.

Drake killed the engine and dropped the car keys into his pocket. "Foot *O D?* Did he overdose on reflexology?" He shot a grin at LuLu.

She returned a deadpan stare. "It says 'foot date.'"

He glanced back at the license plate. "So it does. Guess they stuck a zero in for effect." He winked playfully at LuLu. "Foot date. I guess that's what we had last night."

"A foot date?" She brushed a curl out of her face. "You and I, Drake Bond, seem to do things backward. First we get married, then we have a date. Next you'll be asking me out."

"And after that, you'll flirt with me."

"And after that, we'll make eye contact."

"*Eye* contact?" He made a dismissing sound. "Too normal. We'll meet the way we met—*full-body* contact. You and me tumbling on a hot sidewalk outside a wedding chapel."

"Right chapel—"

"Wrong couple." He wanted to laugh at their whimsy, but he didn't feel lighthearted. Were they really the wrong couple? He'd never know. In an hour or so, after her exam, he'd take her to the hospital and then he'd head back to L.A. It would be bye-bye to LuLu, the quirkiest dresser, funniest lady and best Van Damme stand-in he'd ever met.

Their gazes locked. A distant whir of insects filled the summer day, their buzz mimicking the electricity that coursed through him. He'd been many places with women: swank hotel rooms, balmy beaches, romantic restaurants. But none of it felt as intimate or pleasurable as this simple moment, parked on a street with LuLu.

"Before you go in…" He cleared his throat. Damn, the words felt stuck there. He'd never been this nervous with a woman before. "I'd like to…" *Don't hesitate now, buddy. Be truthful.* "I'd like to kiss you."

Her eyes widened.

He'd insulted her? This was his opportunity to blow it off. Throw out a line like, "Yeah, a smooch for good luck." But he didn't want to be the old Drake—the cocky, truth-dodging, I'm-above-this-love-stuff kind of guy.

He scratched his chin, feeling like a teenage boy fumbling through a first date. "I've never asked for a kiss before."

"You could start out slow—first ask for your scarf back, then ask for a kiss."

"I'm not talking about other women." He gently pressed his finger against LuLu's lips when she started to respond. "Take a moment to filter while I talk, okay?"

She nodded.

He traced her rosebud lips, which were soft and pliant under his fingertips. "After your exam, I'll take you to the hospital. But after that, I'll be returning to L.A. You don't want an involvement. Neither do I. With those odds, I'll probably never see you again." A sadness rocked his insides. It took him a moment to gather his thoughts. "Before I leave your life, I want...I want more than anything to kiss you one last time."

Cupping the back of her head, he moved toward her, observing her reaction. If she didn't want this, he'd back off. Fast. But when she closed her eyes and slightly puckered her lips, a wave of heat that had nothing to do with the temperature rolled over him.

And then he tasted her. Sweet, soft. Just as he remembered at the chapel. His tongue edged along her bottom lip, asking to be invited in. She answered by opening her mouth wider. He slipped inside and searched her warmth and wetness. She tasted like oranges and summer, all sweet and hot.

A small moan escaped her. She returned his kiss with a passion that surprised and thrilled him.

He'd never felt lost in a kiss before. As though his will had abandoned him, leaving behind a swirl of sensations. The electricity of LuLu's lips. The warmth of her ragged breaths. The softness of her hair against his cheek.

With great effort he slowly pulled away. The look in her eyes was his reward: glimmering passion that matched his own. He had never wanted a woman more. Wanted, desired, needed. All of it, the whole package.

But if fate mocked his upbringing, the package included hardships.

He stroked her cheek. A light scent of jasmine trailed past, mixing with LuLu's fresh scent. "You need to go inside."

She nodded weakly. "Come with me while I take my test?" She motioned limply to the building. "It's air-conditioned."

"Cool air sounds good." *A cold shower even better.* He started to open the door, but LuLu touched him on the back, stopping him.

"I have an idea."

He glanced back at her. "One kiss is enough. Another and we'll need a deep freezer to cool us off."

She quirked her mouth. "I'm not talking about sex."

He scrutinized the determined look on her face. Behind those brown eyes, he saw wheels turning. A good dose of passion short-circuited his synapses, but it seemed to kick start LuLu's.

"Should I be scared?" he asked.

"After I finish the exam, let's drop by Capri, the casino where I used to work."

Drake swiped at a bead of sweat that broke from his hairline. "Why in the world would we do that?"

"To, uh, steal some ledgers."

Drake nodded as though what she had said was perfectly clear. "Okay. Then after that, let's hold up a few gas stations."

"I'm serious."

"Now I'm really scared." He wasn't going to kiss her again, that was for sure. For most women, a kiss ignited passion. For LuLu, it ignited her criminal instincts.

Leaning against the car seat, he watched a hawk soar lazily overhead. Lucky bird. It didn't have to be a human being in Vegas helping a woman with a diamond in her gut.

And a scheme in her mind.

"Grave kept a second set of ledgers," LuLu continued. "We'll steal them and use them to negotiate Gramps's and my freedom."

The bird disappeared from view. Which Drake wished this

conversation would. "Isn't it enough that we're evading gangsters?" He lowered his gaze to hers. "Do we have to *steal* something so more people, such as the *police,* start chasing us as well?"

"Look, I have a good reason. During the entire drive over here I was thinking—*filtering*—and I remembered that Grave kept a second set of books. We'll steal them and leave a note saying they'll be returned, along with the diamond, *if* he calls off his thugs and lets me repay Gramps's debt in a timely manner. This way you don't need to play escort, and Gramps and I can return to our home. No more car chases, no more hiding out in Thor's Hideaway!" She smiled as though this escapade was a piece of cake. "You can return to your life in L.A., we can return to our life here."

"We need to get inside. You're suffering from heatstroke."

"I'm suffering from Grave's manipulations and threats."

Although she spoke calmly, Drake heard her fear. It tore at his gut to think about the self-control she was using to keep her wits about her. Although he wanted to say LuLu's idea was crazier than her homemade, sci-fi outfits, the truth was she was reacting to something real and horrific with an idea that was plausible.

He opened his door and stepped outside. But a plausible theory was different than a plausible *reality.* Glancing back at her, he asked, "How do we just walk into a casino and steal a set of accounting books? This isn't an action-adventure movie." He shut the car door.

LuLu opened hers. "I've worked there for ten years. Trust me, I know every side entrance, every stairwell in that place. I know how to slip into Grave's office undetected. All we have to do is find the books—"

"*All?*" They'd be smack in the middle of Grave's territory, in the middle of thugs and guns. Drake blew out a gust of air. "We'd better place our orders for headstones now. One engraved with Drake and one with LuLu."

She slammed her car door. "This is the *only* idea that can save me and Gramps."

Drake kept pace with LuLu as she marched up the curved

driveway to the front door of What's Afoot. He had to admit that he felt a grudging respect for her convictions. And her ability to march in this heat.

"You don't have to get huffy because I don't readily agree to being an accomplice in a crime."

She stopped. Where before he'd seen glimmering passion in her eyes, he now saw flaming fury. "Why don't you leave?" she said icily. "Go back to L.A. I can find another *accomplice*."

She was more hardheaded than a bowling ball. Drake crossed his arms. "Like hell."

She crossed her own arms. "Watch me."

As they stared each other down, he knew damn well she'd find someone else for her latest Van Damme escapade. Probably some fellow reflexology testee. Maybe Foot Date who owned the van with the American flag in the back window. Nothing like a getaway car with no horsepower, thousands of imprints and a national emblem. The gangsters wouldn't need a car to catch them. Just a few advertising leaflets. Have You Seen this Van? Dial 1-800-THUG for Your Reward.

Drake hadn't come this far to have LuLu hook up with some van dude who didn't know the sixties were dead. Who'd all but hand her over to Grave's gangsters.

Well, no wonder LuLu loved action-adventure flicks. In an hour and a half, this woman could single-handedly battle an army, bring about world peace *and* start a new fashion craze. Drake dropped his arms. "You win," he said in a grudging voice. "But after this, no more schemes. Deal?"

LuLu uncrossed her arms and flashed him that impish grin. "Deal." She leaned forward and pecked him on the cheek. "You're a doll. A real hero."

"A hot hero." When she did a double take, he added quickly, "I meant the temperature." He cupped her elbow and guided her toward the front door. "Let's get inside where it's air-conditioned."

Some corner of his brain entertained a vague hope that a blast of refrigerated air would chill further thoughts of stealing ledgers from her mind.

The rest of his brain knew better.

8

AFTER THE TEST, LuLu stepped into the waiting room of What's Afoot. For most of the exam, she'd felt fine. But right before the end, the nausea had returned. Despite bouts of wooziness, she'd completed the questions and hands-on demonstration.

And before she went to the hospital, there was something else to complete—stealing those ledgers.

She glanced around the waiting room, which looked as though it had been decorated by someone who wasn't sure which decade was best: the fifties, sixties or seventies. A framed photograph of James Dean sat angled next to a lava lamp. The early futon furniture, painted bright primary colors, clashed with the paisley wallpaper.

If she hadn't felt nauseous before, she would now.

To center herself, she stared at two oversize diagrams that hung on the wall to her left. One was a foot, the other a hand. On each, cursive black script labeled longitudes and pressure points. Underneath were the words *The Reflex Zones*.

Below the diagrams, sprawled across a lemon yellow futon couch, lay Drake.

The Drake Zone. Her gaze traveled over his sleeping form. No man had a right to look so good in a two-day-old tux. The dress shirt, casually rolled up at the sleeves, had wrinkles crisscrossing the pleats. Another man wearing such a crumpled shirt would look like a slob.

Not Drake. Crumpled and rumpled looked sexy on this man. He could single-handedly put irons out of business.

She walked across the braided oval rug and started to tap him on the shoulder.

"See ya, Lu."

She looked back and waved to a trim guy in blue jeans. "See ya, Alex."

Another man, one with a red bandanna tied around his head, sauntered into the room. "Who's Rip Van Winkle?"

A tall woman with long blond hair that almost reached the bottom of her short skirt joined them. Several of the guys had given Tracy the nickname Whiplash because of how fast she turned men's heads.

She stuck out one hip and eyed Drake. "Not bad. Who's his owner?"

As though on cue, Drake woke up. Glassy-eyed, he stared at the small crowd before shifting his gaze to LuLu. "Every time I wake up lately…" he yawned "…you or a roomful of people are checking me out." He glanced down at his shirt and pinstriped pants. "At least this time I'm not naked."

Tracy flashed a deadpan look at LuLu. "He's *yours?*"

"Mine?"

Staring at Drake, Tracy lowered her voice to a range reserved for smoky back rooms. Pointing a manicured finger at LuLu, she said, "She swore she was through with men. What does that make you?"

Drake dragged his fingers through his unkempt hair. "Chopped liver?" He winked at LuLu. "If she's through with men, she shouldn't have married me yesterday."

"We're not mar—"

"Let's leave the honeymooners," Alex teased, cutting off the rest of LuLu's sentence. Tracy, looking a little miffed, joined the guys as they filed out the front door, leaving LuLu and Drake alone.

"Must have zoned out," Drake said, still looking as though he wasn't sure what planet he was on. "Didn't get much sleep on that hard floor last night."

"Don't change the subject."

He scratched his chin. "Didn't know we were on one."

"You embarrassed me in front of my friends and future co-reflexologists."

"By falling asleep?"

"By that naked comment, followed by that married comment."

"Both are the truth."

She pressed her lips together in irritation. "But you didn't have to blab to them."

"You said they were your friends." He stood and tucked a corner of his shirt back into his pants. "And you don't want them to know we got married?"

"We're *not* married, dammit!"

Stretching his arms over his head, he looked around the room. "Who decorated this place—Jefferson Airplane?" He pointed a warning finger at LuLu. "Don't cuss, by the way."

She opened her mouth in surprise. "Don't—? Now you're stealing my grandfather's lines."

"Speaking of Gramps, let's head back to the motel, pick him up—Suzie, too—then drop you off at the hospital."

"We're stealing the ledgers—"

"I've been thinking," Drake said, raising his voice as though he hadn't heard a word she'd said. "When you're released from the hospital, I'm proposing you two—three—stay at my place till you're well enough to get resettled."

"Stop changing the subject."

He paused. "This *is* the same subject."

"No it's not. We're stealing ledgers, not moving to L.A." She glanced at a clock on the wall. "And now's the perfect time. Grave is a creature of habit—he'll be lunching at one of his local spots." The word *lunching* made her stomach turn. She swallowed hard. "Let's go."

She started to march toward the front door, but a firm hand on her shoulder stopped her.

"I agreed to help you," Drake said, spacing his words evenly, "although I think this caper is crazier than a *Pink Panther* movie." He loosened his hold, but kept his hand resting on her shoulder. "If something goes wrong, however, let's agree that my idea is the backup plan."

She stood stiffly, facing the front door. "This backup plan involves our living in your L.A. bachelor pad until I'm well enough to 'resettle'?"

"Exactly."

She didn't dare turn around. She felt lousy—queasy and feverish. One good, close-up look and Drake would see she felt ill. He'd insist the ledger escapade was off. She tried to sound chipper. "An old guy, a headstone and a chick in your pad? We'll cramp your bachelor life-style."

"Chick?" He chuckled. "You surprise me, LuLu. You wear feminist T-shirts and call women 'chicks'?"

She swallowed again. She had no idea where "chick" had come from. Maybe in her feverish state she was channeling James Dean. Or maybe in the early stages of appendicitis one developed a new vocabulary.

"Anyway," Drake continued, "time I went on a date diet."

"Yeah, you're getting a little fat around the ego." She immediately regretted her words. "Sorry. I didn't filter." But she knew the truth. The little—okay, big—green monster was raising its head. LuLu abhorred the idea of all those women flocking around Drake's bachelor pad like a bunch of wayward pigeons.

"You agree to the backup plan?" Drake asked.

So many pigeons. So little time. If she wanted to sneak into Grave's office now, she had to agree.

"Okay," she muttered, heading toward the door. "L.A. is the backup plan."

A few minutes later, they were in the Corvette and heading back toward the Strip. Fortunately, Drake concentrated on her directions and not her pallor. Eventually, they reached Capri. The gold Chevy wasn't in the large, rectangular parking lot. Neither, LuLu assured Drake, were any of Grave's cars.

"Park on the street, just in case," she warned.

After he'd parked on the road, behind a cluster of palm trees, LuLu jumped out of the Corvette and bolted ahead.

Several long strides and Drake was at her side. "You acted odd all the way over here," he said accusingly. "Are you still upset over my date diet comment? I was kidding, you know."

"I know."

"If we end up in L.A., I won't flaunt other women, if that's what's eating you."

He wouldn't flaunt other women? As though he'd have to make an effort to hold back the pigeon masses!

She spun around and jabbed an index finger at his crumpled shirt. "You think you're—you're *irresistible*. You're not, you're..." Damn him, anyway. She couldn't think of any adjective *except* irresistible.

"What's the problem?" He reached out, but she pulled away.

"Your problem is that you date Sylvia types—all fender and no soul."

But Drake was no longer listening to her burst of anger. Instead, he observed the flush in her cheeks and the glistening in her eyes. Her symptoms weren't totally from rage. He touched the back of his hand to her forehead. She pulled away, but he held his fingers firm against her hot skin.

"You're running a fever."

"In case you haven't noticed," she answered, pulling his hand away from her face, "it's noon hour in Vegas in the middle of summer. The temperature is probably several digits higher than my weight."

Drake gently steered LuLu toward the shade of several large trees that edged the parking lot. In the slightly cooler shadows, he looked knowingly into her face. Into those big brown eyes that never lied.

"Temperature has nothing to do with it. You don't feel well."

She took a shaky breath. "Okay. I'm a little under the weather—"

"I'm taking you to the hospital."

"No, you're not." But her voice had lost its fight. She didn't have the strength to argue. Lightly touching his hand, she said, "I'll be honest. I'm a little nauseous. And probably running a slight fever. I've felt this way all morning. The doctor warned me I'd experience these symptoms for a few days. But I'm not experiencing any other pain, which tells me there's still a little time before I have to go into the hospital. And in that window of time, I *need* to get those books." She blinked back tears. "They're my only hope."

My only hope. He knew what that meant: hers and Gramps's only hope for a normal life, without fear of Grave's reprisals. It was easy for Drake to blow off the ledger scheme. He could return to L.A. and live a normal life. Not LuLu.

"Let's call the cops—"

"Some of them are in Grave's back pocket. I'd run a bigger risk calling the police than sneaking into his office."

He looked up at the swaying palm fronds. He could insist she go into the hospital now. By tonight, Grave would have his diamond—and despite the time delay, he'd probably be able to complete the original gem deal. But Grave would still be on hers and Gramps's case to repay his gambling debt. Even if LuLu started work as a reflexologist in two weeks as planned, it would take years to pay off thirty grand.

If Grave even agreed to a payment plan. After all, he was an addict. To gambling. To money. Rather than wait for debt payments to trickle in, he'd likely force her to sign over her home. And she and Gramps would end up in some cramped apartment, making ends meet. No room to raise a baby, so goodbye to adopting a child.

Thinking of LuLu losing her dream brought back memories of his mother losing hers. From his early childhood he remembered his mother's easy laugh. But after years of hardship, her smiling face had gradually settled into lines of despair, until eventually her features were set with resignation. The thought of that happening to LuLu filled him with an unbearable wretchedness.

"Okay," he said, lowering his gaze back to LuLu's face. "Let's get those books."

It was the way she looked at him—with gratitude shining in her eyes—that cinched some elusive feeling that always seemed out of his reach. At this moment, he felt closer to her than he ever had to any woman. Felt a protectiveness cloaked in tenderness.

"But let's agree on one thing," he added. "We give this adventure thirty minutes *tops*. Then we're out of here."

LuLu frowned. "Forty?"

"Twenty."

She sighed. "Thirty."

They walked across the paved lot to a white door that blended into the whitewashed wooden structure. White seemed an odd color for a gangster's business. Like a bride wearing black.

"It's the showgirls' entrance," LuLu whispered, her hand on the knob. "If anyone sees us, they won't think anything's unusual, because on Sundays they have matinees at two."

She opened the door. Drake followed her inside.

The rush of cool air was invigorating after the withering heat. He stopped and waited for his eyes to adjust to the gloom. Gradually, he deciphered some scattered props and a stage manager's podium. The world behind the show. After all the plays he'd directed, this was familiar territory for Drake.

LuLu nudged him. "This way," she whispered.

He followed her to a narrow metal staircase. The stairs creaked and clanked despite their cautious assent. At the top was a long hallway with several doors on either side. A few overhead bulbs cast soft pools of light on the thickly carpeted floor. LuLu made a beeline to the last door on the right.

Reaching it, she stopped and felt along the edge of the doorjamb. "There used to be a hole where Grave kept a second key," she said under her breath.

Drake hoped she knew what she was talking about because he saw no exit from this deadend hallway. If someone caught them, their only means of escape was back down the noisy metal staircase. Hardly a smooth escape route.

"Yippee," LuLu said quietly, extracting a small metal key. She held it up for Drake's inspection.

"Great. It's a key. Now open the door." He looked back toward the staircase.

They slipped inside. Drake shut the door while LuLu began scouting the room.

"He used to be a guy with simple tastes," she said, motioning around the office. "Just goes to prove that money and taste don't go hand in hand."

Thanks to the light from windows in the far wall, Drake

saw that the room held enough furniture and art objects to stock a small pawn shop. Drake liked sleek furniture and lots of space. This crowded office made him feel claustrophobic.

"Check out that case." LuLu indicated a heavy wooden bookcase in the corner. "I remember he used to stash papers behind the books."

If she'd started out as the wardrobe mistress, eventually becoming the makeup artist, why would she remember where Grave stashed papers in his office? Drake dismissed the thought as he crossed to the bookcase and carefully opened the heavy glass doors. When the light from the windows glinted off the doors, he realized they were set with beveled glass. This bookcase would cost Drake several months' salary, at least.

As he felt behind each shelf, he looked out the windows, which offered a view of the stage below. Several showgirls dressed in street attire were rehearsing a dance step. He imagined Grave sitting up here, observing the show. Probably felt he owned the women—probably treated them like cattle. Drake knew that type of man and it made his skin crawl. When they got out of here, and when LuLu was back on her feet, he'd explain to her that he, Drake Hogan, was not a James Bond clone. That he respected women. Revered them. Hell, he idolized them.

It's just that…he was afraid of commitment. Commitment—marriage—meant hardships.

"There used to be a secret compartment in this desk," LuLu said, interrupting his thoughts. Jiggling a drawer in a massive, engraved wooden desk, she muttered an expletive.

His search complete, Drake shut the glass doors, which closed with a soft click.

He crossed the room as LuLu picked up what looked to be a knife. "This should do the trick," she said under her breath, forcing the tip of an oversize letter opener into a crack below a desk drawer. A sharp snap followed.

"I see we're not going for finesse," he said.

"Voilà!" LuLu wiggled the letter opener, then pulled open a drawer.

"Can't see what's inside," Drake commented, leaning forward for a better look.

LuLu eased both hands into the drawer. "I feel something. It's flat. Smooth. Want to bet it's—" she lifted out a notebook "—the answer to my problems?"

He didn't need more light to see the smile that creased her face. She crossed to the windows and opened the book. Using the light from the stage to read, she flipped through a few pages. "These must be the real ledgers, not the doctored ones he shows to the IRS. Otherwise, why would he hide them in a secret compartment?"

But Drake was staring at a shimmering object left in the drawer. He reached inside and felt an edge of cool, slick metal. Pulling it out, he discovered it to be a silver picture frame. Turning slightly, he held it so the light from the windows illuminated the photo of two people holding each other in an embrace. He pulled the picture closer. Was it his imagination, or did the girl in the picture look familiar?

LuLu was at his side, staring over his shoulder at the photograph. He felt her stiffen. "Put it back," she said, her voice oddly cold. "Let's get out of here."

He stared at LuLu, but with her back to the windows, he couldn't decipher the look on her face. Then it hit him.

"*You* and Grave—?"

The door to the office swung open with a crash. The room flooded with light.

In the blinding brightness stood the Blues Brothers.

Shorty, looking like a lump of coal in a Hawaiian shirt, leered at Drake, then LuLu.

"We hit the jackpot," he said to his tall cohort, who stood behind with the familiar stupefied look on his face. "Diamond Lil and her boyfriend."

Drake prayed LuLu would filter her thoughts and not blurt out, "He's not my boyfriend."

In the following silence, he realized she was learning the filtering technique. He glanced over. Her eyes were opened so wide they took up half her face. Her mouth was slightly open, as though she'd been caught midgulp.

This wasn't a filtered response. This was a frozen response.

Shorty pulled a gun from his holster. "Say byebye boyfriend. We gotta gut Lil for that little sparkler she's carryin' inside."

Gut? Drake had to do something. *Fast.*

"Who's that?" he said, peering at a space behind the thugs.

Tall Thug turned and looked behind him. "Huh?"

Shorty, glancing at his buddy, snorted. "Don't fall for that old trick—"

Drake threw the picture. The silver frame spun across the room. Just as Shorty turned back, the impromptu missile thwacked him on the forehead.

"What the—" He doubled over, the gun clattering to the floor. Blood spurted. Shorty pressed his hand to his forehead while shouting for his buddy to do something.

Time slowed. Drake looked over at LuLu, who was taking huge strides across the room toward Tall Blues. Damn. Frozen one moment, Wonder Woman the next. He yelled, "Stop," but she was on a mission, her curly hair flying behind her, her eyes pinned on Tall.

"Stop?" repeated Tall, looking clueless.

"I didn't yell stop, bozo, *he* did," barked Shorty. On his knees, one hand pressed against his bleeding head, he reached for his gun, which was inches away from his stubby fingers. "Don't stop. *Go!* Get the bi—"

Drake leaped over the desk and dived for the gun. Not a neat lunge. His hand missed the object, which now dug painfully into his shoulder. As he twisted and reached beneath him, something heavy landed on him, its weight forcing the air from his lungs in one painful whoosh.

Panting for breath, he caught a flash of Hawaiian print. The lung-bursting weight had been Shorty.

A thug on top of him. A gun underneath him. *I'm a gangster sandwich.*

He shifted his gaze in time to see LuLu plant a mean kick in Tall Thug's groin. His responding bellow reminded Drake of a moose he'd once seen in a wildlife documentary. For the moose, however, it had been a mating call.

For Tall Thug, it might be the *end* of his mating calls.

"Give me your gun!" Shorty snapped. He stuck a bloody hand toward Tall, who remained doubled over, moaning loudly.

Drake reached underneath himself for the pinned gun. His fingers touched the cool metal.

"Don't pull a fast one," warned Shorty, his gravelly voice close to Drake's ear.

"Too...late," Drake said between breaths. Damn. His finger slipped off the gun, losing the connection. Time for a backup plan. He jammed his knuckles into Short's rib cage. "Tell Godzilla to drop it."

Tap tap tap. Drake didn't have to look to know that LuLu was prancing. The floor reverberated with her impromptu dance.

"That's no gun," Shorty said, a trickle of his blood dropping onto Drake's cheek. "That's your finger, dummy."

Thunk.

Shorty rolled over, moaning, holding his nose. "She *kicked* me!"

Drake grabbed the gun and jumped to his feet.

Tall bellowed another wounded-moose call.

Shorty released a string of expletives.

LuLu continued prancing.

He had to get control of this three-ring circus. "People! I have a gun!" Although why he needed it, he wasn't sure. His sidekick was more deadly than a small arsenal.

Tall, stifling another moan, semistraightened and pointed his gun at LuLu and Drake. "Me...too."

Drake leveled the gun at Shorty's nose. "Drop it, or your buddy's head is gonna look like a smashed cantaloupe." George Raft had said something similar in some bad B flick. Considering the circumstances, it seemed a good line to steal.

"You'd...shoot...Nathaniel?" said Tall between groans.

Nathaniel? "Watch me." Drake aimed at Shorty's head. "Cantaloupe's in season."

Tall dropped his gun. It clattered onto the hardwood floor. LuLu jumped forward and retrieved it.

Drake jabbed his gun in the air. "Raise your hands." For all he knew, these bozos might have more weapons concealed. Although he'd bet Tall wouldn't remember where.

"My nose is bleeding!" Shorty complained, his voice muffled behind his cupped hand. Red blood now mixed with the loud colors on his Hawaiian shirt. "I gotta hold my damn nose!"

"Did I hear 'cantaloupe'?" Drake said.

Tall raised his hands. Still stooped over, he didn't have to raise them high. Shorty grudgingly raised his, exposing the blood smeared across his nose, his forehead and his hands.

LuLu stood next to Drake, holding Tall's gun. No matter how many Stallone and Van Damme flicks she'd seen, he knew she had as much knowledge about handling firearms as he did. Yet here they were, having a pistol-pointing showdown with two gangsters. He'd *never* get married again.

"You two..." Drake hesitated. He was accustomed to delivering ultimatums to raucous students, not damaged gangsters. "You two..." Damn. What else had George Raft said in that flick? Drake shifted mental gears and recalled a Western he'd once directed. "You two have until sundown to get out of town."

Shorty blinked in confusion. Tall remained wide-eyed, staring at LuLu's feet.

Drake backed toward the door, pulling LuLu with him. "Count to a hundred before you leave this room or... Nathaniel's gonna be fruit salad." LuLu had opened the door and was in the hallway. Drake edged out, shutting the door after him.

"Run!" LuLu whispered hoarsely, tearing toward the staircase.

She clutched the ledgers in one hand, the gun in the other. She might be impetuous, Drake thought, but she kept her wits about her when push came to shove.

Or kick.

They clamored down the stairs, sounding like a herd of stampeding moose on a tin roof. When they reached the bottom, LuLu darted toward the back door that led to the parking lot, opened it, but held up the ledgers to signal "stop" when Drake approached.

"This way," she whispered urgently, running back into the darkened backstage area.

Drake glanced toward the opened door. Toward *freedom*. "But—"

LuLu was already on the far side of the stage. Drake followed, knowing the thugs would be barreling down that staircase any moment—they probably couldn't count to one hundred if they tried. Well, one of them, anyway. And even if LuLu seemed to have temporarily lost her sense of direction, it was better they remain together rather than apart.

Because if he lost LuLu again, Gramps would kill him. And he feared Gramps's wrath just as much as two Vegas thugs'.

In the gloom, he followed LuLu's shadowy form. A door opened. A rectangle of yellow light fell across the dusty backstage floor. "In here," she whispered.

Drake jumped inside, blinking at the blast of light. Behind him, the door clicked shut.

"Wonderful," said a throaty-voiced woman who sat with several other women in front of a bank of mirrors. "It's thirty minutes to show time and we're being held up by our makeup artist and some stud."

"I'm the makeup artist," LuLu explained to Drake as she snapped the bolt on the door.

"Oh good. I was worried you were the stud."

Leaning against the door, panting for air, LuLu did a double take at Drake. Together they'd broken into a gangster's office, stolen a set of illegal ledgers, disarmed two thugs and run for their lives. And Drake still had the wherewithal to be witty? Although she felt like one step above roadkill, she couldn't control her burst of laughter. "You pick odd times to show off your sense of humor."

"Have to, if I'm to compete with you."

They were both still smiling, but the sparkle in Drake's eyes also contained a somber message. They could have died up there, but instead they were here, alive. In a crazy way, he meant more to her now than he ever had. As the thought passed through her mind, his gaze intensified as though he knew exactly what she was thinking. A powerful undercurrent of emotion flowed between them, cementing a bond stronger than any vows.

"LuLu, honey," interrupted the woman, "it's difficult enough penciling in my eyebrows. But with two people holding guns behind me, I'm afraid I'll end up looking like Joan Crawford."

LuLu looked down, surprised that she was still holding on to the gun. "Sorry." Rotating the gun so it hung upside down, she looked at Drake, who held his weapon pointed toward the floor. "We need to put these things away...." She heard her own words, but it felt as though someone else was speaking. Her skin prickled with heat. The surge of adrenaline that had helped her survive the last few minutes was depleted, leaving her weak and feverish. She tossed the ledgers on a side table and headed toward a back cabinet. "Let's stash them in the cabinet before we do something stupid," she said between breaths.

Drake followed her. "All we need is for one of us to blow a hole through our big toe." He placed his gun next to hers on a shelf.

"Then there'll be two of us in the hospital," LuLu said. "One for an appendage, one for appendicitis."

He grinned, but she saw a hint of sadness in his eyes. He gently touched her back. "I can't believe you kicked those guys."

"Got strong legs. All that bicycling." She wiped the sweat from her forehead. "Plus I've practiced a few high kicks with the girls during off-hours." She tried to smile, but knew it looked fake. She was scared. And sick. And now what were they going to do?

"It's going to be okay, you know," Drake said softly, rubbing her back. "We'll be out of here soon."

Only Gramps spoke to her in that tone of voice—tender, protective. She missed him. Missed their home. She gritted her teeth, not wanting to cry. When had her simple life become so complicated, so frightening?

She looked over at the long makeup counter underneath the wall mirror. Some of the girls were in T-shirts and jeans. Some were topless, seemingly unconcerned that there was a man in the room. But considering that they paraded around the stage seminude, being nearly naked in front of one man probably didn't faze them.

They were in various stages of preparation for the matinee. Although LuLu's unofficial title was makeup artist, most of the girls liked applying their own. Typically, LuLu helped the new girls or someone who was late. Often she lent a sympathetic ear and some unfiltered advice. Eventually, after the shows, she'd started giving foot massages as well, which led to her reflexology studies.

A trim woman wearing horned-rim glasses and a spiky white hairdo entered from the back. Seeing LuLu, she stopped and squealed, "Baby! We heard about the diamond! I've been so worried about you!" As she ran toward LuLu, not one ounce of her taut, tanned body jiggled. Which was easy to see because all she wore was the bottom half of a string bikini.

"I'm okay," LuLu assured her as they hugged. Pulling away, she motioned to Drake. "Drake, Belle. Belle, Drake."

"Your original ride to the exam," Drake said in a strange monotone.

LuLu looked at Belle's attire, then back to Drake. "Don't worry. Unlike you, she doesn't own a convertible." She looked back at her friend. Summoning more composure than she felt, she explained, "Grave's thugs are after us."

With a brusque nod, Belle said firmly, "You're safe here. We'll think of something." That was Belle. Always a can-do attitude. The night Suzie had died, after Gramps had gone to bed, LuLu and Belle had talked until the wee hours of the morning. To this day, LuLu didn't remember the particulars of the conversation, but she remembered Belle's attitude. Steady. Reassuring. As Gramps might say, "She's a lollapalooza."

Cocking one dark eyebrow that matched her roots, Belle looked at Drake. "He's…?"

"Her husband," he answered.

His voice had an edge LuLu hadn't heard before. If she wasn't mistaken, he sounded downright possessive. Of her? In the back of her mind, she wondered if Drake didn't just *feel* responsible for her, but *wanted* to be responsible.

"Don't start that husband stuff again," LuLu warned, but she'd lost her oomph. Sinking into a folding chair next to the cabinet, she explained to Belle, "I left the back door open. Figured Grave's thugs would run into the parking lot, thinking we were on the loose and not in here."

"So that's why you did the door detour," Drake said. "Good thinking."

"That girl, she's got smarts," Belle said.

"That girl is also on the verge of appendicitis," Drake said somberly. "We need to get her to a hospital."

Belle shot LuLu a surprised look. "Appendicitis?"

LuLu brushed a curl out of her face. "The diamond didn't take a normal path. It's stuck at the opening to my appendix."

"Oh, baby, you never do things the easy way." Belle checked out the wall clock. "Twenty-five minutes to show time. You could take a chance and slip out that back door— but one of the goons is probably lurking around the building." She shifted her gaze to Drake, then back to LuLu. "I have an idea."

Without waiting for a response, she strutted to a rack of sequined costumes and, after pawing through several, pulled out a corseted number with enough feathers to take flight.

"Remember Barbie with the bazookas the size of Manhattan?"

One of the girls chortled. "Barbie Boobie."

Belle held up the feathery number and peered at Drake over the top. "She had hips to match those bazookas. This should fit you."

He looked around. Seeing that no one else responded to Belle, he returned her gaze. "Me?"

"You."

"No."

"Yes."

"No—"

"Drake," LuLu interrupted. "You're sounding like Gramps in one of his stubborn moods. Belle's right—a disguise is our best chance for escape."

Belle marched toward Drake with the outfit and handed it to him. "If you're shy, there's a bathroom in the back." She turned to LuLu. "And you, baby, can fit into just about anything. Pick out something while I finish my makeup."

Drake stood stiffly, staring at the outfit as though it were an alien. "I realize you mean well, but there's no way—"

"Grave's goon-boys know what you look like?" Belle planted one fist on her hip while leveling Drake a get-with-it look.

Drake nodded.

"'Nuff said." She pulled a pair of stockings from a lingerie bag hanging on the rack. "These fishnets should conceal your hairy legs," she said, tossing them to Drake. She looked twice at his feet. "Maybe Barbie had big hips, but you beat her in the feet department."

Another showgirl piped in. "He can't go barefoot. He'll slide all over that stage."

Squaring his shoulders, Drake said matter-of-factly, "I'm not going onto the stage—"

"Wear your shoes," Belle said, cutting him off. "Who's gonna look at your feet, anyway?"

A red-haired showgirl, chomping on gum, said, "Maybe we should help your hubby get dressed." In the mirror's reflection, she winked one thick-lashed eye at Drake.

"I can get dressed by myself, thank you," he said tersely. On the way to the bathroom, he muttered, "I need a toothpick." Minutes later, when he exited from the bathroom, one of the girls gave a low wolf whistle.

"Please," he said under his breath, "just treat me like one of the girls."

"Okay, girlfriend," said Belle. A shimmering, tinsel-layered headpiece covered her Annie Lennox hairdo. The gold fringe matched her outfit—what there was of it. She leaned over Drake and popped open a makeup kit. "Let's get you dolled up, doll."

"Makeup," he said in an unenthusiastic monotone. "Let's just cover the five o'clock shadow and call it a day."

But Belle was already slathering foundation on his face. "Hush. You look like a linebacker in drag, but with makeup you might pass for a big-boned girl." She dipped into the makeup kit and extracted a small circular container. "Close your eyes. Time to make those baby blues stand out."

When Drake opened his eyes again, he avoided the "big-boned girl" in the mirror. Instead, he checked out a showgirl who stood behind him.

Dressed in a low-cut, form-fitting, red-sequined number, she stood behind his chair, peering intently at his reflection. Her face was perfectly made up with arched eyebrows, red lipstick and thick lashes. Her hair, piled on her head in a mass of curls, was secured with a gaudy red clip that matched her outfit.

"LuLu?" he croaked.

"Hi," she answered softly.

He grinned. A big pinch-me-I'm-dreaming grin. "I think you should throw out the rest of your wardrobe and just keep that little number."

"Stop talking," Belle said in a miffed tone. "How'm I supposed to put lipstick on?"

"Let me help," LuLu offered. "After all, I'm the makeup artist here."

"Good." Belle straightened and readjusted her headdress in the mirror. "I made him look okay, but he needs an expert's touch."

The thought of LuLu touching him sent shivers down Drake's spine.

LuLu leaned close with a lipstick tube in her hand. "Cold?"

Hardly. "Why do you ask?"

"You have goose bumps down your arms."

Good thing she wasn't checking elsewhere—she'd see the biggest goose bump this side of Minneapolis. "Just for the record," he said, summoning his most masculine voice, "I've never before worn women's clothing."

LuLu laughed lightly. "I'll never tell." She held up the

lipstick. "I need to put on your lipstick—open your mouth like this." She leaned in and opened her lips wide. Red, soft lips. "Like this," she instructed again.

It took every last ounce of willpower not to open his lips "like this" and kiss her. As she leaned closer with the lipstick, he smelled her sweet freshness. "You are one drop-dead-gorgeous babe," he whispered huskily.

"Bad Boy," she admonished with a frown. "Just like a man to go gaga over a woman's exterior rather than her interior."

He glanced into the mirror and blinked his false eyelashes at his reflection. "Bad Girl, you mean." The goose bumps umbumped. He opened his mouth to say something in his defense, but wearing a corset and makeup just didn't set the mood for a serious relationship talk.

He dutifully opened his mouth.

After slathering on lipstick, she tossed the tube back into the makeup box. "You're just like other men—what's outside is more important than a woman's insides." She grabbed what looked like a beaded doily and tossed it to Drake. "Put this on your head."

He grimaced, fingering the network of interlaced beads.

"It's a hat," LuLu explained. "To cover your manly do."

He smiled, hoping his lipsticked lips didn't disguise his sincerity. "For the record, I don't think what's outside is more important than what's inside, LuLu."

"We're going backstage," Belle interrupted, walking up behind them. "You two join us as we leave the dressing room, then duck out the back door. If you run into a goon, say you're going out for a quick cigarette or something." She looked disapprovingly at Drake's arms. "We should have shaved him. Well, too late. If anyone asks, say he's on alternative hormone therapy." She turned on her heel and walked saucily toward the door. "Chop chop, girls. Time to strut."

Drake wanted to say something more to LuLu, try to make her understand how he felt. Damn, even when she was sick, she was hardheaded.

He felt like one of the cattle as they herded toward the door and filed out into the gloomy backstage area. LuLu, her slim body neatly outlined in red, walked in front of him. To the left, he saw sunlight streaming through the back door they had originally entered.

He'd never thought he'd enter this joint as a man and leave as a woman. Maybe his karma had finally caught up with him.

He grabbed LuLu's hand. "You got the ledgers?"

"Wedged in my costume. It's a miracle I can walk."

He glanced down, wondering…but reeled his imagination back in. Best not to know the particulars. "Let's go," he whispered, pulling her toward the door.

They broke from the pack of showgirls and headed toward the door.

Just as they reached it, Tall Thug stepped from outside and blocked their exit.

9

TALL THUG, backlit by sunlight, was in the doorway that led to the parking lot. Considering he stood erect, Drake guessed he was over his bad Moosie experience.

"You girls is headed the wrong way," he said as Drake and LuLu approached.

Maybe Tall stood tall again, but his voice sounded strangely higher.

LuLu giggled nervously. "Thought we'd bum a cigarette before show time."

"You girls is always bumming cigs." Tall shook his box of cigarettes at LuLu.

She extracted one and held it up between two fingers. "Gotta match?"

"Not since Di Niro," Tall answered.

Di Niro? Why was it bozos always compared themselves to Italian movie stars? Drake was glad he was in the shadows. Otherwise Thug would see his disbelieving smirk.

"What about your galfriend?" Tall flicked his lighter to the tip of LuLu's cigarette. "You bum for her, too?"

LuLu inhaled deeply. "He—she's..." She sputtered and coughed. Smoke flew out of her nostrils and mouth. Another attempt to talk ended in a long wheeze.

"I'm shy," Drake interjected. Damn. He should have practiced his showgirl voice. He sounded like Mel Gibson on cold medicine.

Drake laughed loudly to cover his faux pas, which was another mistake. If Tall Thug had sounded like a wounded moose earlier, Drake's laugh sounded like a neutered elk.

With dread filling his corseted body, he spoke again, this

time sliding his voice to a higher pitch. "I'm, uh, in alternative hormone therapy," he explained, stealing Belle's line.

LuLu continued to hack and cough.

Stepping forward in a patch of hazy sunlight, Drake smiled at Tall Thug. *I need to distract his attention from LuLu.* Drake prayed she wouldn't try to inhale again—it was obvious she'd never smoked a cigarette in her life. So much for a smooth exit. They were stuck playing chit-chat with Moosie.

"Hate to bum cigs from a gentleman," Drake said, finding a falsetto that seemed to work. For good measure, he blinked his false eyelashes.

One stuck.

Tall stared at Drake, who wasn't sure if the thug's dumbfounded look was the norm or a reaction to the Amazon before him. Drake was considering saying he was Barbie Bazooka's older sister when LuLu cut in.

"Right." She cleared her throat. "Shy. So I bum them for her." Her voice sounded strained, as though she'd been sucking helium. She half staggered toward Drake and handed him the cigarette.

"Thanks, girlfriend!" he said in his newfound girly voice. To hell with the months he'd spent wearing patches and gnawing on toothpicks to kick the habit. This was life and death—and he needed a puff. Besides, his damn eye wouldn't open. What had Belle used to attach these lashes—super glue?

As he filled his lungs with smoke, LuLu—coughing slightly—teetered back toward the stage.

With his one good eye, Drake stared down Tall, mentally cursing LuLu for leaving him alone with Thug of the Year.

"Shy, huh?" Tall dipped his head to the side and grinned. Drake wondered how so many teeth fit into such a tiny head. "I like 'em shy."

Drake felt like saying, "And I like 'em smart," but bit his tongue.

"Shy...and big boned," Tall added in a suggestive undertone. He winked, then kept his eye closed.

Great. He thinks my stuck eye is a wink. Drake had never before felt like a piece of meat. How was he going to brush off Di Niro's evil twin? Worst-case scenario, he could try one of LuLu's lethal kicks, but with this damn corset on, he doubted he could raise his foot more than a few inches. Besides, with only one eye working, his depth perception was off. He'd probably end up kicking Thug's big toe.

Hardly a stunning blow.

"What kinda therapy you in?" Thug asked, both eyes wide open.

Wonderful. He's testing a pickup line on me. Drake, who always viewed his *own* lines as top-notch, made a mental note to toss 'em. It felt lousy being manipulated by a bozo with an ulterior motive.

"Alternative hormone," Drake repeated. His eye popped open.

"Hormone?" Tall repeated, leering.

Sucking on his cigarette, Drake glanced back toward the stage. Now that he had twenty-twenty vision again, he needed to find LuLu.

He looked back to find Thuggy staring at Drake's hairy arms.

"Side effect," he explained. "All those hormones. It's a bitch shaving my biceps."

He put his hands behind him, remembering to keep them away from his tail feathers. All he needed was to ignite one of those plumes with his cigarette. Tall might like his women big boned, but he'd be in for an even *bigger* surprise if Drake's costume caught fire and had to be yanked off.

"It's been lovely talking about...hormones and hair," Drake said in a cheery falsetto. "But it's almost show time."

"Wanna meet later for a drink?"

Over my dead feathers. "Don't drink. Can't mix hormones and booze. Doctor's orders." Drake smiled sweetly before taking a long drag of the cigarette.

He exhaled. "Toodle-loo," he said breezily, twiddling his fingers in a goodbye wave. He turned slowly and clopped away.

Damn dress shoes. Drake put a little sizzle in his walk,

hoping it would raise Tall Thug's gaze from checking out his wing tip shoes. But not enough to raise his hopes.

Hearing nothing behind him after several more clops, Drake dropped the sizzle and picked up his pace.

LuLu, lined up with the showgirls offstage, glared at Drake as he approached. When he sidled close, she whispered, "About time."

Drake threw his cigarette down on the floor and squashed it with his heel. "Sorry. Moosie has the hots for big-boned girls."

"Moosie?"

"Tall Blues Brother."

LuLu let her gaze roam over Drake's face, trying to read his expression. Which was impossible considering his features were hidden underneath thick pancake makeup, bloodred lipstick and lashes that could double for awnings.

"You're not taking this showgirl stuff seriously, are you?"

"Do you think they have an opening in the show?" When LuLu didn't answer, Drake cocked one eyebrow. "Look at me. I couldn't take myself seriously if I tried."

"Okay," LuLu said, nervously tugging on a curl. "Plan is for us to stay in the back. Act like decoration. The girls will cover for us."

"In the back?"

"Of the stage."

"I was kidding about an opening in the show—"

A fanfare blasted over the PA system. Several of the girls strutted single file onto the stage, megawatt smiles plastered on their faces.

LuLu fought a wave of nausea. Sweat beaded on her forehead. This was more than stage fright. These were the symptoms the doctor had explained would precede appendicitis. If she asked Drake to take her to the hospital, now, he would. There was just one glitch.

"Nathaniel is prowling the area," she whispered to Drake, averting her head so he wouldn't see how ill she felt. With his growing protectiveness, she feared he'd pull another macho stunt that would attract the wrong kind of attention. And they'd come too far not to play it cool for a few more minutes. "Nathaniel will most likely leave in a few," she continued, fighting to keep her voice even, "and then we'll slip offstage past Moosie."

"With a better line than bumming cigs."

The music surged. Several more girls strutted away. Belle, her gold headdress shimmering under the stage lights, flashed them a get-the-hell-out-here look.

Drake gave LuLu's arm a reassuring squeeze. "We've gotten married, drag raced and played with guns. Being showgirls is a piece of cake." Placing his finger under her chin, he tipped up her face and gazed into her eyes. "Remember, I'll be watching out for us.…" His blue eyes darkened with concern. "What's wrong?" he whispered urgently. "Are you feeling sick?"

Just the situation she wanted to avoid. They were so close to getting out of this mess. One false move now would blow everything. Faking a smile, she forced herself to sound stronger than she felt. "Scared, you idiot. Let's get out there."

He regarded her quizzically for a moment, then nodded. "If you start to feel woozy, lean against the back wall. I'll…" He blinked rapidly. One of his eyes remained shut. "Damn eyelash," he muttered.

"I'll lean against the back wall," she repeated. What did he think she'd do? Jump off the stage?

"Right." His one-eyed gaze traveled over her outfit. "Are the ledgers still…?"

She held her arms out the way she saw the other girls doing. "I tossed them back into the dressing room. Didn't want to chance the papers falling out on stage." She touched Drake's arms. "Hold them up."

He did.

"Try not to look like a walking clothes rack," she whispered before strolling onto the stage. Behind her, a clopping sound followed. Had to be Drake's dress shoes. Hopefully, people would be more enthralled with his big bones than his big shoes.

The lights were hot. Stifling. Like being in the middle of the desert. Turning slightly, she glanced at Drake.

A glob of makeup dripped down the side of his face. He was visibly panting. And she was worried about getting woozy? It would stop the show cold if the big-boned girl keeled over.

LuLu stopped and struck a pose. Her insides were playing spin-the-wheel. She resurrected Drake's words in her mind. *We've gotten married, drag raced and played with guns. Being showgirls is a piece of cake.*

Piece of cake, she repeated to herself. Piece of cake. Cake. *I miss Gramps's chocolate concoctions.* If they got out of this mess, she'd never again gripe about her grandfather's culinary experiments. If they didn't get out of this mess... She imagined Gramps alone, with no one to argue with. No one to cook for.

No one to love.

The last thought brought tears to her eyes. Damn. She couldn't think about the downside of this fiasco—not now. She *had* to believe everything would work out for the best.

She sneaked another look at Drake, who, compared to the other girls, looked like Mount Everest in sequins and feathers. He stood slightly in front of her—probably to hide her. He was obviously trying to mimic some of the other girls' poses, but his tilted head looked as though he had a crick in his neck.

A line of girls sashayed past him. LuLu was horrified to see that, for some reason, he decided to join the strutting girls. Unfortunately, when they all thrust our their arms, his hit one of them on the side of her head. Her elaborate hat, which looked to be part birdcage, slipped to a precarious angle. With the shift in weight, she stumbled and fell on another girl.

Drake lunged to steady the birdcage, missed and landed on top of yet another showgirl. Which brought the collision total to three show girls, one dragster.

LuLu shut her eyes. A piece of cake? More like a piece of chaos. Probably would have been less painful if they'd let the thugs shoot them earlier.

Squeals. Rips. Clops.

In the commotion, no one heard LuLu's groan. She pressed her lips together, fighting the urge to cry out. A hot, searing pain tore through her lower right abdomen. She staggered back a few steps and slumped against the wall.

When the pain ebbed, she opened her eyes. The audience was howling with laughter at Drake thrashing about on the floor with two showgirls. No one had noticed LuLu's episode. Easing in a shallow breath, she checked out the backstage area. No Nathaniel. She looked back at Drake, praying he'd see her. *Soon.*

Drake lifted his head. A shapely leg in a fishnet stocking lay across his feathered stomach. He followed the leg past a silver-trimmed corset to a face contorted with fury.

"You idiot," whispered the showgirl, shoving the birdcage contraption back onto her head.

Another girl, struggling to her feet, glared at him. "You jerk," she mouthed.

On the floor with two gorgeous showgirls. Any man's fantasy. Except these girls weren't amorous, they were furious.

Can that fantasy.

Murmuring an apology, Drake staggered to his feet and tried to get oriented. A sea of faces confronted him, the audience laughing and applauding. His gaze caught someone's in the front row. The man's jaw dropped as he stared at Drake in astonishment.

Russell.

Drake's buddy, for whom he had been best man only yesterday, was sitting in the front row with his bride, Liz. She cocked one eyebrow, grinned and flashed Drake a thumbs-up.

He shrugged apologetically. It would take days, maybe weeks, to explain the misadventure of the last twenty-four hours to his best bud.

Drake turned, searching for LuLu. Behind a few confused-looking showgirls he spied her, slumped against the back wall, clutching her stomach.

He charged upstage. The clops sounded like horse hooves, but he didn't care. Just as he reached her, she crumpled. He swept her into his arms. The audience exploded in applause.

They think this disaster is part of the show.

He just hoped Nathaniel and Moosie, if they'd witnessed any of it, thought the same.

Holding LuLu close, he carried her beyond the curtains. Backstage, he stopped and stared across the room to the door that led outside. Sunlight streamed around a form blocking the doorway. Tall Thug. Because of the darkened backstage area, Drake knew he couldn't see them.

"Hold on," he whispered to LuLu. "We have to deal with Moosie again."

She nodded. "Don't..."

"Don't what, honey?"

"Don't flirt. I might get jealous."

He gulped back a laugh. "Now's not the time for humor," he said solemnly. Sane advice from a man who looked like Willard Scott in a tutu. He headed toward Moosie.

As they approached the door, Tall Thug stared at them in surprise. "Did the cig do her in?"

"The cig?" Drake said in a girly voice. "Yes, the *cig*. She got dizzy. Tripped. Hurt her foot. I need to take her home."

"Hurt her foot, too?" Tall's gaze went from LuLu's high heels to Drake's cloppers. "Those look like—"

"Slippers. Leather bedroom slippers. I always wear them when...I'm carrying my friends." It would take Tall at least a day to figure that one out. Drake shifted LuLu in his arms. "It's been lovely, but gotta get Shirley home to soak her foot."

"Shirley?" Tall asked, squinting into LuLu's face. "I don't remember a Shirley—"

"Yeah, Shirley," said a brazen voice behind them.

Saved by the Belle.

She stepped in front of Drake and LuLu, her gold tinsel headdress luminous in the sunlight. "Shirley's a new girl," she explained in a no-nonsense tone. "And so's her friend. We were trying them out in the show."

She turned and gave them a knowing look. "I think you forgot the sheet music," she said, handing a manila envelope to LuLu.

The ledgers. "Thanks, girlfriend," Drake said. "We'll need those to practice our steps." He smiled sweetly at Moosie. "Which we can't do until Sally—"

"Shirley," Belle corrected.

"Right. Shirley," Drake repeated, "gets her foot fixed." Holding LuLu, who gripped the stolen papers, he eased past Tall and Belle. His feet had just hit the asphalt when someone pinched his behind.

"Hey!" Drake barked in his normal voice.

He glanced back in time to catch Tall grinning lasciviously at him. "Come back after you drop off Shirley."

Drake's glued-shut eye popped open.

Tall winked back. "I like big-boned girls."

Drake winced, turned and made a beeline for the 'Vette. "Don't look back," he instructed under his breath. "Act normal."

"Me?" Leaning against him, LuLu choked back a laugh. *"You're* the one dating Moosie."

"We're not *dating,*" he said defensively. "Unlike you and Grave."

"You're jealous," she said, her words muffled against his chest.

"I'm not—" He stopped himself. *Yes I am.* He was a greener shade than LuLu after inhaling cigarette smoke. "It's this damn corset," he said defensively. "Can't think straight. Your history with Grave is your business, even if I do think he's a—"

Her soft fingers touched his lips, cutting off the rest of his speech. He looked down. Her big brown eyes glistened with fever.

He picked up his pace. "Hang on, honey. You'll be at the hospital soon."

Clop clop clop. LuLu shifted her gaze skyward. With every one of Drake's steps, palm trees shook against the pale blue summer sky. She felt woozy, and worse, the pains were taking hold. Painful jabs shot through her lower right side. Before she got sicker, she wanted to set the record straight, because after she went into the hospital, she might never see Drake again.

"Grave liked...exteriors more than interiors," she said between breaths. "Didn't matter that we were engaged—he was still fender shopping."

"Engaged?"

"Yes. He treated my heart recklessly. Never again." She stifled a groan as another pain seared through her.

Drake picked up the pace. "Damn. We didn't want to park in the lot because it's too close. But the street seems like another country...."

"I can walk."

He held her closer. "No. I'm taking care of you."

"Just as you did—" she slowly released a breath "—for your sisters...."

"No, just as I do for the woman I..."

Even in her pained state, she was aware of his incomplete thought. The women he what? *Loved?* Not the type of confession Drake Hogan would make. She must be sicker than she thought. Or maybe his corset *was* too tight.

They reached the car. He lowered her over the passenger door into the seat, then bounded around to his side. After he jumped in, she murmured, "Thank you."

He jammed the key into the ignition. As the engine started, he said with conviction, "LuLu, I'll never be reckless with you—or your heart." They pulled away from the curb.

She nodded as though she understood, but didn't. Since it took most of her energy to fight her pain, any leftover strength was better spent doing *anything* but analyzing his words. Because if she let them, his words would haunt her forever.

Fifteen minutes later, they careened into another hospital parking lot. Despite her intensifying abdominal pains, LuLu had been able to give clear enough directions to get them to the hospital. But by the time they pulled up outside of the emergency entrance, she was doubled over, groaning.

After slamming to a stop, Drake jumped out of the driver's side and ran around to her door. Yanking it open, he scooped her into his arms and carried her inside. As they approached the admitting desk, the clerk eyed them over the top of her reading glasses.

"She needs a doctor, *fast*," said Drake, fighting the panic that surged within him. "She's having an appendicitis attack."

With a quick scan of Drake's attire, the clerk motioned to a wheelchair next to her desk. "Let's put her in the chair." She stood and reached toward LuLu.

"I can handle it," Drake said, carrying her to the chair. "Call a doctor." Lowering her onto the seat, he murmured, "You're going to be okay, honey." But when their gazes caught, he could see that she wasn't so sure. Her brown eyes, watery with pain, questioned if she'd make it. After all, people sometimes died when their appendix ruptured.

Squeezing her hand, he winked with a lightheartedness he didn't feel. "You're going to sail through this—after all, you're LuLu Van Damme, action-adventure star."

"I think I've had a little too much action lately," she whispered hoarsely.

Drake gestured to his corset. "Join the club."

Her grin was undermined by a moan. Clutching his hand, she squeezed her eyes shut.

"Can we get some medical attention here?" Drake said to the clerk. He forced himself to speak calmly so as to not frighten LuLu, but his insides were screaming, "Help her, dammit!" Time moved slowly, too slowly. Every moment LuLu was in pain felt like a small eternity. If he had to, he'd pick her up and carry her to an operating room, to a doctor, to wherever she'd get some help.

Just as he was ready to drop the modulated-voice act and yell for help, a male nurse appeared. "Let's wheel her to a room," he said cheerfully, gripping the handles on the back of the wheelchair. If the nurse hadn't seemed efficient and knowledgeable, Drake would have decked him for his attitude. What was this cheerful bull? Didn't he know that LuLu's health, her life, were in jeopardy?

Drake squeezed LuLu's hand. "You're going to be fine—" But the nurse pushed away the wheelchair before he could finish.

Straightening, Drake eyed the exiting wheelchair. "Is she going into the operating room now?" he asked the clerk, but his question competed with an overhead paging system. He wanted until the anonymous voice stopped.

"Is she going straight into the operating room?" he repeated quickly, not wanting to be drowned out by the paging system again. LuLu disappeared as the nurse pushed the wheelchair around a corner. LuLu, gone. Something inside of Drake jolted loose, as though an important piece of him was gone, too.

"No, they're taking her to a room." The clerk glanced at him over her reading glasses. "They'll prep her there for surgery and—"

"I need to be with her," Drake said, cutting off the rest of the clerk's explanation. He was vaguely aware of the woman saying something as he jogged across the room, following the path of the wheelchair. He nearly collided with a teenage boy wearing spiky hair and an earring in his nose.

"Watch it, lady," the kid snarled.

"Sorry." Barely slowing his jog, Drake waved an apology to the boy, whose face went from contempt to astonishment.

Behind him, Drake heard, "Awesome rags, man."

After rounding the corner, Drake skidded to a stop and looked down the stretch of hallway. Nurses. Doctors. Beyond two orderlies conversing, he spied the male nurse pushing the wheelchair through a door. *LuLu.* Drake speed walked after them. Reaching the door, he slowed down. Inside, the male nurse was giving instructions to another nurse, while a third stood next to LuLu, asking questions and writing on a form attached to a clipboard.

"LuLu," Drake said, weaving his way through the nurses. Placing one hand protectively on the back of her head, he looked at the nurse with the clipboard. "Can't you ask me those questions? She's hurting."

The female nurse lowered her notes. "I had to get her insurance information," she responded evenly. "Hospital protocol."

LuLu looked up, her eyes fringed by damp curls that clung to her forehead. "You're here," she said softly.

The look on her face, part pain, part surprise, tore at his gut. "After all we've been through, you think I'd miss this?" He tried to smile, but knew he failed miserably. Emotions hammered his insides. He felt raw, edgy, ready to pummel anybody who got in the way of LuLu's well-being.

"You don't need to be here," she continued. She started to say more, but stopped, a look of anguish compressing her features.

"Can't we get her into surgery *now?*" Drake asked the group of nurses. "She's in pain!"

"It's going to be all right, ma'am—sir," the nurse with the clipboard answered. "Are you family?"

"I'm...her husband."

Her gaze dropped the length of his feathered-and-sequined ensemble before she met his eyes again. "Fine," she said in a voice that was anything but. "Stretcher will be here momentarily."

"Stretcher?" Drake repeated.

"To take her into surgery."

Relief coursed through him. She'd be in surgery soon. "It won't be long now," he assured LuLu, gently rubbing the back of her neck. She leaned toward him, indicating that she needed to say something privately. He lowered his head.

"They don't know about the diamond," she whispered. "Make something up...."

He knew what she was getting at. The doctors and nurses were going to be plenty surprised to find a diamond wedged at the opening to her appendix, so there had to be some explanation. But if they knew the real story, they might call the police, which was the last thing this drama needed.

The creaking of wheels distracted him. Shifting his gaze, he saw an orderly pushing a gurney into the room. Under his breath, he said to LuLu, "Don't worry. I'll make something up—and I'll get back the diamond." A shadow of relief crossed her face.

"Time to get you into a hospital gown and onto this gur-

ney,'' the male nurse explained in that cheerful tone Drake
had grown to loathe. The cheerful nurse and the nurse who'd
taken the insurance information helped LuLu from the wheelchair.

Drake closed his hands into tight fists. He didn't like the
male nurse touching LuLu—didn't matter that it was his job,
he was a *man*. Where before Drake had wanted to deck the
guy for his attitude, he now wanted to deck him for being
male.

''Let's get this smock on her,'' said one of the female
nurses.

Drake turned his back as they undressed LuLu. He recalled
how earlier—was it really this morning?—he'd brazenly
checked her out in her cartoon undies. But that had been different; she'd checked *him* out first. Now he wanted to give
her privacy because she was vulnerable. Fragile. Attributes she
probably despised, thanks to her Van Damme mentality. But
despite her bravura, he knew a part of her would always be
the introverted little girl playing make-believe with Mayberry.

''Okay, let's go,'' one of the nurses said.

Drake spun around. The orderly was pushing the gurney,
with LuLu on it, through the door, back into the hallway. In
two steps, Drake was at her side. ''I'm here,'' he said softly,
taking her hand. He looked into her pale face, constricted with
pain. ''You're going to be okay,'' he added, hoping his voice
sounded more assured than he felt.

He brushed a lock of damp hair off her forehead. She looked
up at him, those big brown eyes blinking sleepily. They'd
probably given her a shot of something. He squeezed her hand.
''Hang in there, Van Damme.''

One side of her mouth quirked. ''Don't cuss,'' she whispered.

He fought the urge to laugh. Wasn't that like LuLu—finding
humor in the middle of a crisis. That's what he wanted for the
rest of his life, a woman with wit. And spunk. And although
she'd deny it, fragility...

''You can't come in here, sir,'' said the orderly.

Drake looked up. They were in front of two swinging doors

on which were stenciled STAFF ONLY in large block letters. The operating room.

He looked back down into LuLu's big brown eyes. This was it, the last moment before she went into surgery. He touched her face, not wanting to lose her even as he knew she had to go. "LuLu, I—" But she slipped past him as the orderly pushed the gurney through the doors, which swung open, then soundly closed.

Drake stood alone, his fingers poised in midair, still feeling the softness of her cheek. "I love you," he finished under his breath.

10

"SHE LOOKS SO FRAGILE." Drake stood at the foot of LuLu's hospital bed, watching her. The operation had been a success. LuLu had been back in her room for several hours, sleeping. Late afternoon sun filtered through the blinds, streaking the linoleum floor with bands of light.

"She *is* fragile," Gramps whispered. He sat next to the bed in a chair, his big hands folded in his lap. "She might act like Van Damme, but inside she's Doris Day."

"Doris Day?" Like Gramps, Drake knew LuLu had her soft side. But he'd never compare her to a fifties' movie star with a strange hairdo. LuLu was a nineties' woman. A Meg Ryan. But hardly a Doris—

"What's wrong with Doris Day?"

"Nothing." Drake stepped to the other side of the bed and gently swept a wayward curl off LuLu's forehead. "Just that LuLu has spunk."

"Doris has spunk, too," Gramps said defensively. "Didn't you ever see *Pillow Talk?*"

Drake wondered if these were the kind of conversations Gramps and LuLu had at home. If they debated movies and stars, he could definitely hold his own. "You're right. Doris had—has spunk," he conceded. If Suzie was spoken of in present tense, he'd better give Doris the same due. Drake gave his head a small shake. "Van Damme and Doris Day," he murmured. "Exteriors versus interiors."

"Eh?"

Drake ran his hand along the bed's cool metal railing. "LuLu and I talked about a person's exterior and interior. She accused me of liking women for the former and not appreciating the latter."

Gramps reached over and adjusted the sheet. "That's LuLu, all right. Calling a spade a spade."

"Or a fender a fender." Drake looked down at her serene face. "Never thought I'd see a moment of peace after everything that happened these last few days," he said quietly. "But now that LuLu's health is on the mend and Grave has backed off, we'll be spending a lot of peaceful moments together."

He was tempted to pull one of the roses from the bouquet he'd purchased at the hospital gift shop and leave it on LuLu's pillow. The delicate scent of the flowers reminded him of the cologne she'd been wearing when they'd first met. Or first tumbled, he thought with a smile.

He was reaching toward the bouquet when Gramps spoke. "I need to talk to you, son."

Drake looked at him, surprised at the older man's pale appearance. Concern? Fear? Dr. Yarberry had repeatedly assured them that LuLu would be fine.

Which meant something else was worrying Gramps.

"Grave is out of the picture," Drake assured him. "Thanks to our stealing those ledgers, he's promised to leave you two alone."

Gramps scratched his chin, which had sprouted a short white growth. They had managed to shower, dress and pack before they left Venus, but a razor hadn't touched either of their faces in several days.

"Grave's no longer a problem," Drake said with finality. But even though his words were meant to soothe, Gramps continued to stare at him strangely.

"No, he's not a problem," Gramps said solemnly. He puffed out his cheeks before continuing. "You're the problem."

Drake blinked. "Wearing a corset was *not* my idea."

Gramps sighed heavily and shook his head. "Last night, when you were helping LuLu with her reflexology exam, I wasn't asleep the entire time."

Last night. It seemed like days ago that he and LuLu had

confessed their fears…as well as their affection for each other. Sitting together in the shadows, they had felt free to open their hearts. It had been a *private* conversation.

With a jerk of his hand, Drake motioned for Gramps to follow him.

When they were several steps away from the bed, Drake met Gramps's eyes. "You spied on us?"

Gramps puffed out his chest. "Spied? Never!" He frowned so hard his bushy eyebrows merged into one. "I woke up. Heard you say you're not the marrying kind. And some other gibberish." He sighed deeply. "Tried not to listen. Honest, son. But there was hardly any place to escape, unless I hot-footed it to the bathroom."

Drake looked across the room at the sleeping LuLu. She'd been hurt, she'd explained, and didn't want to go that route again. He'd been hurt, too, but in a different way. End result: she didn't want to get married because it meant a life of loneliness. For Drake, it meant a life of hardships?

He tore his gaze away from LuLu and back to Gramps. "What is it you want to say?"

The older man's gray eyes bore into Drake's. "I want you to leave my granddaughter alone."

"But I'm going to marry her."

"We figured you'd get an annulment."

We? Drake glanced over at Suzie's headstone, sitting primly in the corner, before looking back at Gramps. "Rudolpho and Harriet got married, not us. We were the wrong couple, which is why we need to remarry—I mean marry." He made an dismissing motion with his hand. "Forget Rudolpho and Harriet. *I'm* going to marry *LuLu.*"

"Have you asked her?"

Now it was Drake's turn to pause. "Not yet, but—"

"You think she'll say yes?"

Drake swallowed before answering. "I hope so." A cold uncertainty lodged in his gut. This was a twist he didn't like, being nervous about whether a woman would accept his proposal. A position Drake Hogan, the former professional bachelor, had never been in. He'd always been the one dodging a lady's proposal.

And one man's, Moosie's, but that was a small technicality. "I mean, I know so. LuLu will say yes."

Gramps nodded sagely. "I see. And what if you change your mind? Decide a life with LuLu means a life of 'hardship'? After all, you're not the 'marrying kind.'" He looked down at the floor, then back up. "You're the type of man who drives a flashy car named after an old girlfriend. What LuLu needs is a man who drives a family car named for her."

Drake dragged his hand through his hair. "I think I'm being judged rather harshly by a third party."

Gramps gently touched Drake's shoulder. "True, you're being judged...by a grandfather who loves LuLu more than anything on this earth. I've seen her crushed by a man's mistreatment, and by damn, I'd rather go to hell than see her destroyed by another's."

Gramps's vehemence astonished Drake. He felt humbled before this man who so openly—and ferociously—loved his granddaughter.

"Therefore—" Gramps dropped his hand "—I'm asking you to leave LuLu alone. Let her find love with a man who can return it, wholly."

Drake felt as though he was being buffeted about in some stormy sea, unable to steer a clear course. He wanted to articulate his need for LuLu, his hopes for their life together, but his thoughts tumbled and spilled over each other. "I'll—I'll come back later."

"No, son." Despite Gramps's determined tone, Drake caught a wounded look in his eyes. "Don't come back at all."

In all the plays Drake had directed, all the life situations he'd witnessed, he'd never seen such a powerful display of love for another human being. He wanted to argue that he was the right man for LuLu, but he knew nothing—*nothing*—could convince Gramps. LuLu's grandfather had overheard him say, "I'm not the marrying kind," and that had sealed Drake's fate.

But he couldn't leave. If Gramps had overheard words spoken from Drake's fears, he also needed to hear words spoken from Drake's heart.

"Gramps, I'd never hurt her. Or mistreat her. That's my vow to you *and* her. I'd spend the rest of my life loving her—"

"Sorry to interrupt this tender conversation," said a male voice.

Drake spun around. Leaning in the doorway was a man with jet black hair that matched his black tailored shirt. His close-set eyes and protruding nose gave him a wolfish appearance.

The man in the photo. *Grave.*

He stepped into the room. With a commanding air, he looked around until his gaze landed on the sleeping LuLu. "I see Kitten survived the operation." Narrowing his eyes, he shifted his gaze to Gramps. "Where's the diamond, old man?"

Drake stepped in front of Gramps. "I have it."

Grave looked surprised, then laughed. "Drake, I assume? Kitten's boyfriend?"

Kitten? For slimes like Grave, life was one long string of "Kittens." Drake's stomach curdled at the thought of this scum having ever been close to her.

He stepped toward Grave. "Let's go outside and discuss this—"

Grave put out his hand, exposing a gold Rolex watch on his wrist. "Not so fast." Looking at Gramps, then Drake, he slowly crossed his arms. "Let's talk deal."

"You and I already talked 'deal' on the phone," Drake answered.

"Oh, *that* deal." Grave waved the arm with the Rolex in the air. "Right. Where you play hide-the-ledgers and I play stay-away-from-Kitten."

"A man of his word," Gramps murmured.

Ignoring Gramps's aside, Grave focused his beady eyes on Drake. "Let's up the ante. Make it more…fun." He strolled to a painting of trees that hung on the wall opposite LuLu's bed. "Hospital art," he said drolly. "Do those pastoral settings really exist?" He tossed a sarcastic look over his shoulder. "Or just in some flaky artist's mind?"

If Drake didn't feel disgust for Grave, he might have felt pity. It was obvious the man didn't appreciate life. People and things were objects to be used or ridiculed.

Grave turned back around. "Fun," he continued, "is upping the ante."

"There's no ante to up," Drake countered. "Unless you want the ledgers to be delivered to the D.A.'s office."

"I know, I know," Grave answered in a petulant tone. "If anything happens to you, LuLu or Gramps, the ledgers will be mailed to the D.A.'s office. I understand your terms, Drake, even though your threat sounds like something out of a forties' movie."

It was. The same George Raft flick Drake had stolen a line or two from earlier. But he wasn't about to confess to stealing lines and plots from old films.

In an exaggerated gesture, Grave touched his index finger to his forehead. "I have a better idea. Let's go double or nothing."

Neither Gramps nor Drake responded.

"Come on, Gramps," Grave goaded, "you're a gambling man."

"Not anymore," Gramps answered defiantly. "You encouraged me to gamble, knowing I needed the money to finish Suzie's..." He cleared his throat, covering the break in his voice. "And you gave me credit when I was losing. By the time I was in deep, I didn't know what had hit me."

It dawned on Drake that Gramps had never said the word *headstone* when it came to Suzie. The old guy was clearly in denial. He couldn't quite accept that his beloved wife was gone.

It was a love that went beyond death.

Drake glanced at LuLu. For the first time in his life, he understood such love.

"Double or nothing?" Grave clicked his tongue as though he could taste the bet.

Drake hated gambling. Had always refused to bet, even on friendly football games. Deep down, he supposed gambling on anything—whether it be with his heart or his money—had been a way to avoid risk, to prevent hardship. But for LuLu's sake, he wasn't going to play it safe anymore.

"Double or nothing?" Drake said, looking pointedly at Grave.

A self-satisfied smirk creased Grave's face. "Do I hear a taker?"

"Talk."

Grave flexed his hand as though itching for the bet. "You got the ledgers. But I'm still owed a diamond. And Kitten and I still gotta negotiate how she plans to pay off the old man's debt."

"You bastard—" Gramps started toward Grave. Drake stopped him with a firm grip on his arm.

"Let's listen," Drake said calmly.

"I'd take his advice," Grave said to Gramps. "This could be the deal of your life."

They might be talking a "deal," but Drake knew Grave was capable of taking more than money. If pushed, Grave would take a life.

Drake could feel Gramps shaking—from rage, not fear. Drake felt that same rage, but knew he had to keep his head.

"So," Grave continued smoothly, "here's the deal. A game of poker. Five hands. Top three wins."

"Wins what?" Drake asked evenly.

Grave rolled his tongue in his mouth as though the words were sweet to taste. "If I win, I get the diamond back. And LuLu and I negotiate how she'll pay off the sixty grand—"

"Thirty," Gramps corrected.

"*Sixty,*" answered Grave sharply. "The game is double or nothing."

"If I win?" Drake asked.

Gramps shot him a sharp look, which Drake ignored.

"I?" Grave echoed. He touched his finger to his forehead again. "We have a taker, I believe."

"No way in hell," said Gramps to Drake, jerking his thumb toward Grave. "Nobody's gambling with this snake—"

"And if I win?" Drake repeated, overriding Gramps's impromptu speech.

"If you win—" Grave's lips pulled back in what Drake assumed to be a smile "—I forget the debt."

"And the diamond."

The smile faded. "Diamond's mine, no matter what."

"Thought we were playing double or nothing. Or aren't you a gambling man?"

Grave paused, just as Drake thought he would. Gambling was in Grave's blood. The thrill of a bet probably ranked higher than a thousand Kittens.

"If I win," Drake said, taking the initiative, "no debt. Plus I keep the diamond *and* the ledgers. The last is nonnegotiable because it's LuLu and Gramps's only insurance that you leave them alone."

Grave's eyes narrowed until they were slits.

"It's a great deal, Grave," Drake said smoothly. "At worst, maybe you lose one diamond. And a small gambling debt. But win or lose, you avoid a prison term because the IRS will never know you kept a second set of books—as long as you forget about LuLu and Gramps, that is."

Moments passed. In the silence, the only sounds were the squeak of nurses' shoes along the hallway's linoleum floor.

"Deal." Grave's voice was barely above a whisper.

"No!" Gramps barked. He grabbed Drake's arm. "No more gambling. It's caused enough problems." He looked at LuLu, his eyes red rimmed. "My baby wouldn't be here if I'd minded my own damn business and never gambled." He looked back at Drake. "I'm begging you, son, don't. Learn from my mistake. Just leave. Go back home. I'll figure something out—"

"He's accepted," said Grave in a self-satisfied tone. "We have a gentleman's agreement."

"You're no gentleman," Gramps said ominously. "You're a—"

"People, that's enough." Drake stepped between Gramps and Grave. The last thing needed was one of Gramps's surprise assaults. "I've accepted." He turned to Gramps. "If I lose, I'll handle the debt. Don't worry."

Gramps looked puzzled.

Drake lowered his voice. "I have money in savings. For college."

"No—"

"No," interrupted Drake, "I've already decided. And I refuse to combat your stubbornness." He smiled. "Tell LuLu I love her."

Gramps's chin quivered. "I'm sorry...."

Drake knew what was coming. Clasping Gramps's arm, he whispered gruffly, "I deserved to hear my own words. It's no way for a grown man to live, afraid of hardship. You taught me a valuable lesson."

Drake turned to Grave. "Let's go."

A NURSE POPPED HIS HEAD into LuLu's hospital room. "Your husband's here," he said cheerily. "Said he'll be in in a few minutes."

"Husband?" LuLu asked in surprise, but the nurse had already disappeared. Turning in the wheelchair the nurses had helped her into—they insisted she ride and not walk out of the hospital—LuLu flashed a confused look at Gramps. "Husband?"

"Rudolpho?" he suggested uncertainly.

LuLu tugged on a curl. "But you said he went back to L.A."

Husband. She started as the realization hit her.

"Your stitches hurt?" Gramps was at her side, gently touching her shoulder.

"No." LuLu grabbed her grandfather's hand. "The man who claims he's my husband..." She shuddered. "It must be Grave."

Gramps's hand tensed under hers. He murmured an epithet that would have made Suzie blush.

"He wants the diamond," LuLu continued in a strained voice. "And his money." She looked up at her grandfather, whose face was etched with worry.

"I was hoping," he said quietly, "that it was taken care of."

"Hardly. Debts like that don't disappear." Her heart

pumped madly, anticipating what was to come. "I have to face him sooner or later. Might as well be now." She drummed her fingers on the wheelchair arm, the soft thumping competing with her racing heart. "I'm starting the new job in a few weeks. I'll give him a percentage of each paycheck. It'll take forever, but the debt—plus interest, no doubt—can eventually be paid. The doctors have the diamond, right?"

When she didn't get a response, she looked up. Gramps, obviously agitated, was chewing on his bottom lip. "Did I say that?"

She stopped drumming. "Don't tell me you sold the diamond and gambled the money, hoping to raise enough to get us out of this mess?"

"No!" His face flushed with indignation. "There was no way in hell I'd have left you alone, Cupcake. And for the record, my gambling days are over."

"Then where's the diamond?"

"I—I don't know."

"Don't know?" Either she was suffering from the lingering effects of medication or reality was losing its edge. She took a calming breath. "You don't know or—"

"I lied." He moved over to the hospital bed and sat down heavily. He ran a hand over his face, as though to erase what was happening. "I just kept hoping that everything would turn out okay, so I told you the doctors had the diamond and that Rudolpho had left for L.A."

"His name's Drake. And Grave's going to walk in here any moment. 'Fess up."

Gramps leaned his hands on his knees and looked at her squarely. "Grave showed up while you were still out. Offered a deal. Double or nothing. Rudol—I mean Drake—accepted."

"Double or *nothing?* Drake detests gambling!" She gave her head a disbelieving shake. "While I was sleeping, all three of you were in my room, playing high-stakes let's-make-a-deal?" Reality hadn't just *lost* its edge, it'd gone *over* the edge. "Explain 'double or nothing.' In twenty words or less."

Gramps scratched his scraggly beard. "Five hands of poker,

best three win the ledgers and the diamond. Debt was rene-
gotiated to…'' He winced.

"To?'' she prompted.

"Sixty thousand.''

It was as though someone had drained every last ounce of
energy from her body. "Sixty thousand,'' she repeated slowly.
Not that thirty thousand was small change, but *sixty?* Grave
had played hardball. And as she well knew from past experience, when he did that, the deal was set in concrete.

She looked over at the hospital nightstand, upon which
stood a vase of roses and Mayberry. From across the room,
she could barely make out the three small figures in the center
of her make-believe town. But she knew they were there, just
as her dream of adopting a child was always in the back of
her mind.

"Bye-bye baby,'' she whispered to herself. A sixty-
thousand-dollar debt effectively wiped out that dream forever.
The flowers now smelled sickeningly sweet. She felt Gramps's
big, warm hand on the top of her head. The gesture was meant
to comfort, but it only added to the burden she felt.

"You'll have the money to adopt and raise a baby. Drake
paid the debt.''

She jerked her gaze up to meet Gramp's eyes. "Where did
Drake get that kind of money?''

"From his savings. For school.''

"For his schooling? He gave up his dream in order to bail
me out of my problems?'' Tears crowded her eyes as she gave
her head a shake. "That's not right. I'll pay him back instead
of Grave.''

Outside, down the hospital hallway, she heard approaching
footsteps. Not the squeak of nurse's shoes, but the heavy slap
of leather soles.

A man's footsteps.

LuLu's insides chilled.

Grave.

It didn't matter if Drake had given him his sixty thousand
dollars—Grave wouldn't rest until he'd gotten his precious
diamond, too.

"Where's the diamond?" she asked, her voice barely above a croak.

"Cupcake, I honestly don't know."

No time to debate the location of the gem. No time to do anything but be a family. Reaching over, she took Gramps's hand. "It's okay," she said calmly, as though comforting a child. "We've been through a lot together. We can make it through this, too."

The footsteps stopped.

The door creaked open.

LuLu squeezed her eyes shut. *I still have Gramps. I might lose everything else, but I have my family.*

She opened her eyes.

"Drake." Her voice choked on the single word. Her eyes traveled over neatly creased khaki pants and a white pullover that made his tan look bronzed. When she looked back into his warm blue eyes, he winked.

"Better leave, son," Gramps warned. "Grave is on his way here."

LuLu gulped back a nervous laugh. "Babaloo, I think Drake won let's-make-a-deal. Grave won't be showing his face again."

Drake grinned. "Only if he wants to play quadruple or nothing."

LuLu's face hurt from smiling. Her side hurt from the operation. She'd never felt happier.

"No debt...no harassment." She squeezed Gramps's hand. "We can start living our lives again." She gave Drake a mockingly stern look. "You were willing to gamble away your college education." She wagged her finger at him. "And you call *me* impetuous."

"Well, accepting a bet is one thing," Drake answered in a teasing tone. "Swallowing a rare diamond is another."

"Touché." She smiled. "So solve the mystery—where's the diamond?"

"Want to guess?" Drake asked.

"You swallowed it?" Gramps suggested.

Drake rolled his eyes at the older man. "No." Looking back

at LuLu, he quirked one eyebrow mischievously. "I'll give you a hint."

"Is it larger than a bread box?" she asked, repeating the question Drake had asked when she'd first confessed to swallowing something.

A smile teased his lips. "Smaller." He jerked his head toward the hospital nightstand. "Go look in Mayberry."

LuLu did a double take at the make-believe town. "You mean a rare, expensive diamond has been sitting in Mayberry all this time?" She fumbled with the arm on the wheelchair. "How does one start this thing?"

Drake crossed to the chair and took hold of the handles. "*I'll* do the driving." He pushed LuLu the few feet across the linoleum floor to the nightstand and halted. She stared intently into the small wooden town. "I don't see any diamond...." She picked up the church and looked underneath it. She turned a tree upside down and shook it. Expelling a perplexed breath, she scrutinized the miniature wooden objects again. After a moment, she gasped in surprise. "There's a—a fourth figure in there."

She looked up at Drake. "There are four people in my town," she said in amazement. Looking back, she tilted her head one way, then the other, checking out the new piece. "That fourth one," she said thoughtfully, "isn't shaped like the others. Looks like he's a different wood, too—"

"Does he fit in?" Drake asked. But another question lingered in his voice.

LuLu froze, then she looked from the figure to Drake. "You...it's you."

"It's him all right, but where's the diamond?" Gramps barked from across the room.

"I like to view myself as a diamond in the rough," countered Drake, never moving his eyes from LuLu's. She'd seen that look before—it was how he'd stared at her right before she was wheeled into surgery. It was a look filled with longing and regret.

"Took me a long time to grow up," Drake continued, "to realize what I wanted in life." He fished in his pants pocket, extracted a small box and placed it in her hand. "And here's the diamond Gramps is looking for. I hope it never again gets you into any trouble, that it only brings you happiness."

LuLu turned the soft, velvet-covered box in her hands before opening the lid. On a cushion of blue satin sparkled the pinkish red diamond, set in a shiny gold band. "It's...a ring."

"An engagement ring," Drake clarified. "For the woman I love."

Love. The word he'd left unsaid when he carried her from Capri to the 'Vette. Warmth spiraled within her. *He loves me.* But even as she experienced a surge of exhilaration, her insides caved in.

Drake dropped to one knee and took her hand in his. "Will you marry me, LuLu?"

"I thought you two were already married," Gramps said grumpily, crossing his arms.

"Babaloo, please hand me a tissue?" LuLu asked, blinking back tears. She needed a moment to think. The last few days had been a whirlwind of life-threatening activities.

And this felt like another.

With Gramps's attention diverted, LuLu whispered to Drake, "What about a life of hardship?" She kept her head bent, unable to look into his eyes.

"Hardship?" he echoed. "I've watched you weather some horrendous ones these last few days, and you not only survive, you flourish." He interlocked his fingers with hers. "If for some reason you outlive me, you'll be fine. It's the Van Damme in you."

Gramps returned with a tissue. "Don't cuss."

Taking it, LuLu dabbed at her eyes. "But you have a life in L.A.," she said to Drake. "A future as a child psychologist."

"I don't need to live in L.A.," he answered. "And as far as kids are concerned, I'll need a few to practice my child psychology on." He paused. "Look at me. I want to read your soul in those big brown eyes."

With great effort, she met his gaze.

"What about a life of loneliness?" he prodded gently, his eyes searching hers.

Loneliness. It had been anything but that these last few days. This guy could have bailed out at any moment, yet he had stuck by her. Could it be that after what they'd been through, they could face anything together?

"I see the wheels turning, but I don't hear words," Drake said, tightening his fingers around hers. "But I won't pressure you, LuLu. Tell me to go away and I will."

She didn't want him to go away. But did she want him to stay? "I'm filtering," she said, explaining her silence. It was one thing to contemplate her past loneliness. But it felt infinitely worse to contemplate a future loneliness—a life without Drake Hogan.

"Don't go," she blurted.

His blue eyes darkened with emotion. "I'm on my knees, holding hands with LuLu Van Damme, the most unique, strong and lovable woman in the world. I don't think I'm going anywhere—unless she wants me to."

"I want you to stay," she whispered. "I think a LuLu Van Damme deserves a James Bond, don't you?"

"James Bond?" Gramps echoed. "Thought his name was Rudol—I mean Drake." He gave his head a shake. "Son, you not only have a flow problem, but a name problem as well."

"That's what's wrong with the world today," Drake said, not missing a beat. "Too many names and too much flow." He winked at LuLu.

"Now, let's look at what's right with the world." Drake eased the ring out of the box. "Beautiful, isn't it? Diamonds with such a distinctive red tone are rare." He turned it in the light. "It's a heart-shaped fancy cut, also rare. See the luster? That's the light from both the inner and outer surfaces."

"Where'd you learn so much about precious gems?" asked LuLu.

A sexy grin curled one side of his mouth. "Grave told me. Or that's what I think he told me—it's not easy to understand someone who's speaking through clenched teeth."

She giggled at the image of Grave being bested.

"But it's significant for another reason," Drake continued.

"Because I carried it around inside of me?"

"Exactly," Drake said solemnly. "To me, it will always represent your internal beauty, which matches your external beauty. You can spend the rest of your life looking at your ring, realizing that I love you through and through."

Through and through? LuLu closed her eyes, letting the words wash over her. This was the man she'd accused of choosing fenders over soul, and here he was telling her how he loved all of her. She opened her eyes and stared at the sparkling, red-tinged stone. "I'm guilty of the same thing I accused you of."

Drake frowned slightly. "What?"

"I judged you by your fenders."

"So I'm more than just a pretty face?"

"A lot more."

"Do I take that to be a yes?"

A small, tenacious part of her wanted to hold on to her doubt. But when she glanced at her grandfather and saw the tenderness filling his eyes, then glanced at Drake and saw the love in his, she knew her answer.

"Yes."

"To the woman who bowled me over." Drake slipped the ring onto her finger. "I love you," he repeated softly.

LuLu fought hard to keep her composure. In a shaking voice, she said, "I love you, too."

From his kneeling position, Drake leaned forward and pressed his warm lips against hers. Her insides turned liquid as she returned his kiss. Desire curled through her, accompanied by the pleasing knowledge that they had a lifetime to indulge and satisfy it.

"When you two come up for air," Gramps said gruffly, "Suzie and I have a question. Who are Harriet and Rudolpho?"

Epilogue

"HARRIET AND RUDOLPHO?" Ms. American Gothic crooked her penciled-in eyebrow. "How many times are you planning on getting married?"

Drake donned his most charming smile, the kind he formerly used on irate girlfriends. "Just once more. This is our last stop at Last Stop for Love."

She didn't smile at the play on words.

Crossing her arms, she gave LuLu's form-fitting dress a once-over. Although LuLu had wanted to sew her own bridal gown, there hadn't been time. So one of Drake's wedding gifts had been a bias-cut satin gown—something fitting, he'd explained, for Meg Ryan in a film like *French Kiss*. He didn't elaborate that Meg, all spark and tenderness, reminded him of his wife-to-be.

Ms. Gothic stared unabashedly at LuLu's flat tummy. "Congratulations. You had your…"

Drake and LuLu exchanged glances.

"Yes," answered Drake.

"No," said LuLu at the same time.

"Yes and no," Drake said breezily, putting his arm around LuLu. He flashed another grin at Ms. Gothic's frozen look of surprise. "We were faking it before, just to see what it's like. But soon we'll start working on the real thing."

The front doors opened, interrupting the awkward moment. Sunlight spilled across the faded gold carpet as in strolled Russell and Liz. Arm-in-arm with Liz was a sweet-looking older woman.

Drake waved at them. "Buddy, you made it!"

Walking over, Russell gave his head a disbelieving shake. "Nice to see you dressed in a tux again."

Drake smoothed his hand over his silk, pinstriped tie. "Nice to be in a *fresh* tux for a change. I was a fashion nightmare for a few days."

"I don't know," Russell said with a sly grin, "you were pretty cute in that feather number." Turning serious, he added, "Glad you tracked us down before we left Vegas. I wouldn't have missed this wedding for the world."

"I'd like to introduce my fiancée," said Drake, drawing LuLu into the conversation. "Honey, this is Russell, my best friend—and my best man."

"I've heard a lot about you," LuLu gushed, shaking his hand warmly. She motioned across the room to Belle, who appeared to be giving makeup pointers to Ms. American Gothic. Belle's white-and-silver fringed dress matched her spiky, frosted hair. "That's my maid of honor, Belle."

Drake noted how Russell didn't raise even one eyebrow hair. Being married to Liz must have made his friend immune to flamboyant vixens, he decided.

"Belle's no longer working at Capri," LuLu said in an aside to Drake. "Fed up with Grave's tactics, she quit right after the show. Fortunately, she has a career opportunity in Wyoming."

"They need showgirls there?" Drake asked.

"No." LuLu giggled. "She inherited a diner. Figures she can learn to cook in the time it takes to drive from Vegas to Cheyenne."

Flash!

The older woman with Russell and his bride lowered her camera. "It's recorded!"

Liz, encased in a peach-colored minidress that complemented her blazing red hair, stepped forward. "This is my Auntie, who dropped by our hotel on her way home from a convention." Liz leaned toward LuLu. "I hope you don't mind that we invited her," she whispered. "She believes in taking photographs on significant days."

Auntie tucked the camera into the pink handbag that

matched her pink suit. "Now it's official," she said pertly, smiling at LuLu and Drake. "You two will share a long and happy life." Seemingly satisfied with her mission, she wandered off.

The front doors opened again. In walked Gramps, his six-four frame shrink-wrapped in an out-of-style suit. His white mass of hair stuck out almost as much as Belle's.

Seeing LuLu, he smiled sadly and headed toward her.

"Sorry I'm late, Cupcake. On the way over, I dropped off…" Reaching the group, he stopped and nodded toward everyone. Running a hand through his hair, he continued in a low tone to LuLu, "I dropped off the headstone to Suzie. It was finished, you know."

She gently touched his hand. "I know, Gramps. It's time to…to let go."

"Right. Time to let go. No sense holding on.…"

He made an elaborate display of clearing his throat, but LuLu guessed it was to cover his inability to continue talking.

LuLu had always known that this day would come—she just didn't think it would coincide with her wedding day. She pecked Gramps's cheek. "It's a good day for new beginnings," she whispered into his ear. "I'm sure Suzie loves the headstone." She knew, because he'd loved his wife so much, that he wished he and Suzie had gone together. What had he once said? "That's what's wrong with the world today—Gabriel doesn't blow his horn at the right time."

He squeezed her hand. "My precious granddaughter, on her wedding day." He looked over at Drake and frowned. "This makes how many times you and Rudolpho have gotten married?"

"Gramps, his name's Drake, and this is our first—well, second wedding.…"

She was contemplating how much more to explain, *again,* when she noticed her grandfather's eyes lighting up. "Look at that pink suit. The color of Suzie's headstone."

LuLu looked over at Auntie, who stood primly by herself across the room, staring at the Elvis-on-black-velvet painting.

"That's Liz's aunt. Why don't you go over and make her feel welcome?"

Gramps tugged on the worn sleeves of his suit jacket. "How do I look?"

"Like Prince Charming," she answered softly.

As he made a beeline for the older woman, LuLu knew why Gabriel had waited to blow his horn. Maybe her grandfather had some more living, and loving, to do.

LuLu returned her attention to Drake, who was explaining their first run-in to Russell and Liz.

"You two had just driven off on your Harley, when this vision in lace and rhinestones—" he chucked LuLu under the chin "—bowled me over."

Russell rocked back on his heels. "Warned you, didn't I?" He shot Drake a questioning look. "But how did the professional bachelor say 'I do' only a few minutes later?"

"I'll tell you the whole story some night over a chilled bottle of Chenin Blanc."

"Only one glass," Russell quipped. "I don't want to wake up with another tattoo." He winked at Liz, then glanced toward the filmy gold curtains that offered a hazy view of Strip traffic. "Speaking of names, I didn't see Sylvia parked outside."

"Traded her in for LuLu, a family wagon."

LuLu stared at Drake, surprised. "You traded in your beloved Sylvia?"

His blue eyes glistened. "It was time to put Sylvia where she belongs—in the past. My life now is with my beloved LuLu."

Piped-in organ music filled the room. Behind them, Ms. American Gothic opened the doors.

"See you in the chapel, my friend," Russell said, patting Drake on the back. He and Liz joined the others as they headed inside.

"You have the right license?" LuLu whispered.

Drake patted his jacket pocket. "Let's hope with the right names." Flashing the sexy grin she'd grown to love, he steered her toward the doors. "At least we know it's the right chapel."

"And this time, it's also the right couple," LuLu finished, keeping in step with her husband-to-be.

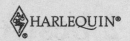

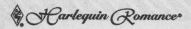

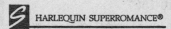

Take 2 bestselling love stories FREE

Plus get a FREE surprise gift!

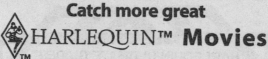

LOVE & LAUGHTER™

**Humorous love stories
by favorite authors and
brand-new stars!**

These books are delightful romantic
comedies featuring the lighter side
of love. Whenever you want to
escape and enjoy a few chuckles
and a wonderful love story,
choose Love & Laughter.

Love & Laughter—always
romantic...always entertaining.

Available at your favorite retail outlet.

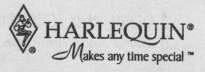

HARLEQUIN®
Makes any time special ™

Look us up on-line at: http://www.romance.net   HLLGEN